earthgirl_

earthgirl_

Jennifer Cowan

Groundwood Books
House of Anansi Press
Toronto   Berkeley

Groundwood Books / House of Anansi Press
110 Spadina Avenue, Suite 801, Toronto, Ontario M5V 2K4
or c/o Publishers Group West
1700 Fourth Street, Berkeley, CA 94710

We acknowledge for their financial support of our publishing program the Canada Council for
the Arts, the Government of Canada through the Book Publishing Industry Development
Program (BPIDP) and the Ontario Arts Council.

ONTARIO ARTS COUNCIL
CONSEIL DES ARTS DE L'ONTARIO

Library and Archives Canada Cataloguing in Publication
Cowan, Jennifer
Earthgirl / Jennifer Cowan.
ISBN 978-0-88899-889-7 (bound).–ISBN 978-0-88899-890-3 (pbk.)
I. Title.
PS8605.O9252E27 2009   jC813'.6   C2008-905688-4

Cover photo by Tim Fuller
Design by Michael Solomon
Printed and bound in Canada

For Alexander

Acknowledgments

For their encouragement, friendship and insights, huge thanks to Tim Smith, Stella Harvey and the Whistler Vicious Circle, Ann MacNaughton, Cynthia Macdonald, Anna Stancer, Robbie Rosenberg, Karen Freedman, Julie Lacey, Douglas Coupland, Amy Stulberg, Bronwyn Cosgrave, Rolph Blythe, Shelley Tanaka, Sarah MacLachlan, Patsy Aldana, the rocking team at Groundwood Books and the Ontario Arts Council.

To Mutti for the typewriter, Grammy for the sense of humour, my dad for teaching me to kick ass, and my mom for letting him.

one_

It was just after the freakish summer of humidity and hail-stones, around the time that the cows got mad again and the chickens went crazy. One of those September afternoons made for skipping the scarring effects of school and healing with your grrlz.

Maybe even kick it up with some retail therapy, if you were so inclined.

"Relax, Sabine, Somerville isn't even here today, so it's not like anyone will miss you," Carmen Vanucci said in the conspiratorial shout-whisper that was my best girl's trade-mark. As if shopping during school hours was actually something to be encouraged.

"Except us if you don't ditch, too," Ella added with her best moony look perfected after years of staring into reflective surfaces (reflective, ha!).

True to form, our moody English teacher Ms. Lesley Somerville was away again. No doubt another messy reac-tion to her latest meds. Or internet date. Or both.

"You of all people know we'll learn way more if we go to Kensington Market," Carmen said. "It's a seething petri dish of humanity, unlike this cesspool of losers."

"Tempting, but I think I'll pass," I said.

"C'mon, Bean," Ella sighed, tugging gently at my sleeve. "It won't be the same without you."

"Yeah, who'll give the running commentary on our every purchase?" Carmen mocked.

"I rode my bike," I said, as if that would qualify as a legit excuse to not ditch and head downtown.

"So, get it on the way home," Carmen said, leaning in close. "Besides, we don't just want you there. We *need* you."

Ella beamed and nodded as they locked arms, stepped closer and ganged up on me. The tough-love slutz.

"Tell you what. I'll rep us for English and meet you at 4:30. By the burrito place," I said, heading down the hallway toward class despite the magnetic pull in their direction. "Later, chiquitas."

• • •

I should have gone with them. Our perma-sub slug Mr. Mendoza's incoherent ranting combined with the lack of air circulation in the class nearly left me comatose. Were it not for staring at the back of Shane McCardle's beautiful babydreaded head and imagining myself gently combing out the gnar-gnar nest of tangles, all might have been lost.

The second the final bell went, I bolted to hot-pedal it downtown.

Within a few blocks, it was apparent I was a tad overdressed in my reflective nylon cycling jacket. But as a safety-first kinda gal, I opted to sweat and be seen. And really there's nothing quite like neon green and reflector tape to ensure you don't blend in with the background scenery.

The traffic was its usual snarly mess. Full-on rush hour, even though it wasn't really rush hour. Actually, it seemed like there wasn't even rush hour any more, just constant traffic tangles 24/7. Suddenly there were more and more cars occupying less and less space in the city. Then again, maybe trying to negotiate the mayhem without being squashed beneath the wheels of a semi or getting the door prize as someone winged their car door open into me made me more aware.

When I finally got my licence, I'd be a way more conscientious driver than these wingnuts.

I was pretty close to exhausted, not to mention beyond sticky and damp, when I cleared the intersection at College and Spadina. What was I thinking, riding down here after another hellish day of school? Though I was salivating for a spicy yam and chicken burrito.

So, even though I knew it wasn't proper cyclist etiquette, I decided to head south on Augusta, which yes, I know, is one way north. But hey, it's not like I'm not cautious and nimble on my two wheels. I would watch for pedestrians, as per the rules of the road, especially since, well, I was going the wrong way.

And really, was my wrong-way pedal more offensive than, say, that suburban she-monster in the scrunchie idling her champagne-colored minivan up ahead in the clearly marked No Parking zone? I think not. Ever heard of greenhouse gas emissions, lady? The disappearing glaciers and ozone? And really, I'm no slave to fashion, but let's not even start on the eons-over scrunchie.

Beside the stupid minivan, Carmen and Ella were already

11   **earthgirl**

at the burrito place, hanging out the swing-out window, meaning they hadn't waited for me.

I took a quick glance down at my watch. It wasn't even 4:30. Now I'd have to eat and walk as they did their –

THWACK!

There was a sharp popping noise and suddenly something soft, dark, gooey and wet was dripping down my face onto my jacket and top.

"Geez!" I huffed as I squeezed my brakes too hard, nearly taking a header over my handlebars.

What had just happened? Had I hit something? Or someone? Won the door prize? Been shot?

I looked around me with that strange super-fast yet ultra-slo-mo sense that seems to take over in situations like this. Up at the cloudless blue sky, at the sidewalk where a pocket dog in a plaid jacket was yapping wildly, down at the brown slime across my chest, then at the ground where I saw crumpled nugget and fry boxes and a drippy synthetic sauce container.

In the minivan beside me, scrunchie skank was wiping her mouth with one of those industrial strength napkins and redoing her lipstick.

And then what had hit me, hit me. The bitch had beaned me with the debris of her McFatty meal!

Almost instinctively, I picked up her crap from the pavement and tossed it back through her open window.

"Excuse me, ma'am? I think you dropped something," I heard myself say in a calm, not the least bit hostile or sarcastic voice.

Wiping the goo of leaked plum sauce off my fingers, I was about to ride away toward Carm and Ella when the littering lunatic flew out of her car and pushed me. And despite, or maybe because of, my bike being straddled between my legs, I keeled over. Right on my butt!

"Now that was not very nice," I screamed, boiling up with a rage I'd never felt before. A rage so big I could feel it in my belly, fingertips, toes and even my ears.

"Look what you did! You got grease and sauce on my interior," she huffed back. "This car is two months old and you ruined it!"

"You threw garbage at an innocent passerby. I think you ruined it yourself, you nutcase," I hollered back, looking around at the street signs and slowly building group of gawkers. "And besides, this is a Loading Only zone and I don't think that means loading your face with food in your big fat polluting car!"

"For your information, mouthy girl, you weren't supposed to be there," she said, pointing at the One Way sign.

"And that makes throwing your crap into the street okay? The world is not your garbage can, lady. And how could you not even see me? I practically glow in the dark here. And then you push me? There are witnesses, you know. I could have you charged with assault, you and your big stupid truck car," I wailed, feeling enraged and exhausted and exhilarated all at the same time.

"Oh, you little radical, riding your bicycle so smug and healthy. You think you're better than me? That you can judge me?" she howled, climbing back into the minivan and slamming her door. "You and your people disgust me!"

And then she floored it, bombing straight through the Stop sign and was gone.

"You could have killed someone, you crazy crazy-person!" I screamed into the air after her.

"With her garbage? Gross, but not exactly deadly," Carmen said as she and Ella suddenly appeared through the small crowd that had gathered, handing me a damp, grotty-looking rag.

"No, running the Stop sign, being a selfish idiot." I plunked down on the curb beside my bike. "Not caring. And what's with the *my people* crap?"

"See, if you'd come downtown with us like you were supposed to, none of this would have happened – or at least not to you, anyway," Ella said, inspecting the spot on my shirt. "I hope that glop didn't wreck your top. I love that color on you."

"You're right," I realized. If I'd skipped with them, I'd have already eaten my burrito and the loon would have chucked her crap on the street uninterrupted. Unwitnessed. Unaccountable. And this whole fabulous fiasco might never have even happened.

Except it did.

"Hey, way to go," a guy with a soul patch and a bull piercing said, giving me props as he walked past.

"Isn't that the truth," an older woman dragging a gro-cery-stuffed bundle buggy nodded. "You certainly told her. Sadly I don't think she was listening."

"Thanks," I smiled, feeling a little awkward and a lot chuffed that these total strangers were congratulating me.

"That was totally insane!" Carmen laughed as she slapped me on the back. "If I didn't video it, I'd have never believed it."

"Yeah, you were pretty great," Ella agreed. "Hey, lock your bike and come inside. We have the best table ever."

"Front row seats, though I doubt anything as exciting will happen now," Carmen said as they hooked arms with me and pulled me to my feet.

• • •

"I might be too revved up to eat," I said as we stood at the counter. I was feeling very zingy and a tad odd, a mix of adrenaline and anxiousness.

"Don't be stupid. You should celebrate," Carmen said. "With extra hot sauce."

The burly counter guy with full arm tats handed me a burrito. Even before I said what I wanted.

"Yam and chicken, right?" he smiled. "My treat, for nailing that whack job out there. My customers can do without sucking back car exhaust."

"Thanks," I beamed. I mean, recognition and free food? It was almost like being a celebrity or something. And all for simply doing the right thing at the right time. Wow.

"We ordered for you before," Ella leaned in to whisper, snatching away my fleeting moment of glory.

"That was so awesome, Bean," Carmen giggled.

"Yeah, you were so crazy, I thought you'd kick her car or slap her or something," Ella said, her eyes widening.

15   **earthgirl**

"Me, too," I answered while stuffing my face. So much for too hyper to eat. I was suddenly famished. "I hate when people are so obviously wrong and act like what you did was more wrong than them to take the heat off or excuse it!"

"You *were* riding the wrong way on a one-way street," Carmen pointed out unhelpfully.

"So, I was on a bike. Besides, that's not as bad as hurling garbage out your car window at an innocent stranger. Not even close."

"Maybe not exactly," Ella said calmly. "Still, they're both sort of wrong, illegal even, and who's to say what's more wrong, especially when you decide you're the one who is right? I mean, of course I'm on your side, Bean, but wrong is wrong, right?"

I stopped chewing for a split second to look at my friends. My supposed best friends on the entire planet.

First off, I couldn't believe that such sentient words and ideas were coming from shiny happy Ella of all people. They were actually almost deep. And secondly, I was amazed at how quickly I'd gone from being the shit to being subjected to a stupid debate on morality. That hardly seemed fair considering I was the one covered in plum sauce. And all they did was stand on the sidelines with their fresh, crispy loot and sparkly new cellphones.

"Wrong, shmong, who cares about any of that? Look at how amazing the picture is on this phone. The resolution rocks. I'm so glad I bugged my mom to buy it for me," Carmen announced. "Check this, you can practically see steam come out of your ears when she pushed you over. Unbelievable."

"What a cow," Ella laughed, leaning into Carmen's shoulder to watch on the minuscule screen. "And in a scrunchie and sweats! Ewwww."

"You filmed all that? Lemme see," I said, grabbing the fuchsia cellphone from her perfectly manicured mitts. I was curious to see how I looked on the teeny tiny monitor, especially since this was a permanent document and all. Who knew, if it were any good, it might even be worth YouTubing. To enlighten and inspire everyone out there in the big wide world.

I seriously hoped I looked kinda cute and a bit hot.

b e i n g h e r e
[September 26th | 10:39pm]
[mood | determined]
[music | PJ Harvey — Good Fortune]

Yeah, yeah, it's been a while for the Bean. Grand apologies all around. I just didn't want to bore you with the minutiae of the minutiae. Guess I was waiting for something epic and explosive to report.

And today that *IT* happened!!

Riding my bike through Kensington Market I got PELTED by some soccer-mom-she-ho and the detritus (thx Mr. Thesaurus) of her mccrappy meal. I FREAKED, as would any normal sane person, since getting pelted with garbage isn't just gross, it's profoundly NOT ON.

What followed was a blur of bad words (mostly mine!), hoots and shouts from bystanders – all caught on video by my girl CV. Click the YouTube link below!!!!

It was a shocking, unnecessary and profoundly horrible event. One I wouldn't wish on anyone. And yet I emerge from it not only unscathed (save for a nasty brown sauce stain) but strangely enriched. Empowered even.

To do better and be better because clearly there are a lot of people out there who need role models and guidance.

And maybe just maybe this happened because I'm the one to inspire the confused, misguided and/or slovenly masses to better, kinder interactions with their fellow beings and beans. Here's to trying anyway.

Inspiringly yours, Sabine the being.

link   post comment
www.youtube.com/watch/W3515z.garbageassault

two_

"Honey, I was thinking, I'm just not comfortable with you posting your picture all over the web for the whole world to see," my mom said at breakfast the next morning.

"Relax. It's not a porno site. It's just video sharing, like that creepo Australian hug-me guy you thought was so adorable," I said.

My mom Rachel, unfortunately, was actually vaguely tech savvy, having somehow, despite her vintage, mastered the skill of text messaging to stay on the down lo with my stupid sister Clare. That and she worked in PR and marketing and was now totally into web stuff. *The future of all interaction and communication*, her colleagues liked to say, as if they had actually invented it or had a clue and weren't led by the hand by their way more clever kids.

"I don't care, I don't like it. Take it down, please," she said with a that's-final-so-don't-argue-with-me tone.

"C'mon, Mom, maybe Sabine just wants some free hugs," Clare goaded. "It could be her only chance to get a cuddle."

"Shut up," I snapped, realizing I was definitely touchy about my neverending boyfriendlessness thing.

19   **earthgirl**

"Don't overreact, Rachel," Dad said as he filled his car cup with coffee. "It's not like anyone's going to bother to watch her have some boring argument with someone. People are busy."

"Gee, thanks for the support," I huffed. "I have a life-changing encounter that might actually be of value to other people and all you do is knock it."

"We're not knocking anything, sweetie," Mom said, now pulling out her sensible-mom voice. "I just don't see the necessity of making an uncomfortable personal exchange with someone into some big public tirade. It's nobody's business but your own."

"Did you even hear a word I said last night? This uncomfortable exchange, as you call it, is about something much bigger. It's like a metaphor for the way people crap on the planet and each other and the animals, on the air, on everything! And it has to stop. Someone has to make it stop."

"Someone has to make this stop. I'm trying to eat the most important meal of the day and this is really annoying," Clare groaned as she shoveled back a mouthful of cereal and made a face at me.

Typical. My supposedly supportive family stomping on my moment of glory. I was actually amped to get to school for once to see how my epic exchange was shaking down in my own personal peer-mediated universe. Who knew, maybe this would surpass Alexis Shaw and her eating disorder in the Northern Collegiate food chain of daily dish.

Even if my family failed to hear it, this was my wake-up call. The beginning of something potentially huge. The way people treated the planet mattered. Pollution, destruction, corruption and greed mattered. Not that they hadn't mattered before, exactly. Just not to me.

How else could you explain garbage in the face! It was so obviously obvious. And I, Sabine Olivia Solomon, could no longer pretend I was more interested in hair extensions and fake eyelashes than the real world. The real, living, breathing and now choking-on-the-crap-we-throw-out-there (through car windows or otherwise) world.

Someone had to step up and speak for the planet and the trees and the water and the animals. To give them a voice. And even if mine was only a little whimper, I had plans to make a whole lot of noise.

"Fine," I sighed. "You go back to eating, shopping, idling the car and consuming till you fall over. Maybe if you're lucky nothing will happen. But don't get on my head because I see that this is about something bigger and actually means something."

"That's my girl. You rant and rage till the cows come home," Dad said as he kissed me on the hair, having clearly not absorbed even an iota of what I'd just said. "And be a sport. Take down the video thing after school, okay? For your mom."

• • •

"Gotta say, Solomon, you surprised me with that little outburst of yours."

I practically skidded to a stop at the husky drawl of Shane McCardle, an elusive sound rarely heard by most and never heard by me. Then again, I rarely heard the sounds of any smokin' guys, unless you counted the nonstop jabbering of Carmen's lunkhead boyfriend Darren Mankowsky.

"Thanks," I stuttered, wondering if he meant good surprised or bad surprised and also amazed he actually knew my name.

"Yeah, had you pegged for one of the clones," he nodded with a raised eyebrow as he loped away. "Dare to be different."

And just like that he was gone again, the knotty head and vibrant blur of his Guatemalan jacket blending into the crowd down the hall.

"That was Shane McCardle!" Ella bolted toward me, practically knocking me over. "What did he say?"

"Nothing, really. Same as everyone else," I lied.

This morning's journey across the lawn and through the front doors had been definitively different from most days. A slew of nods, winks and props mixed with scoffs and the occasional slag greeted me. Even the generally absent (in all senses) mousy Somerville gave me big ups, saying she saluted my "moral indignation."

"You and Shane McCardle. That so rocks," Ella sighed, clearly imagining Shane and *her*.

"He just said hey," I shrugged, though admittedly I was a bit frazzled and electric he'd done even that.

"Looks like you're e-famous," Carmen said matter-of-factly, looking around at the other students as if they were her subjects. "You should milk it while you can, cause sadly fame, especially your kind, is fleeting."

"I'm not interested in fame," I scoffed, feeling a tad outraged that my profound life-changing experience was being distilled down to something so trivial.

"You have so much to learn about playing the game," Carmen sighed. "Why do you think I posted it in the first place? To help you out, get you to the next level."

"Of what? What happened yesterday meant something."

"I'll say," Ella grinned. "You're on YouTube and not having a pillow fight or something pervie like the one Alexis and her posse posted. The skanks."

"No, that we should be paying attention to the world around us. It's in crisis, stressing out."

"No offense, Sabine. But there aren't a lot of people we know or hang with who care about the planet being stressed. We've got enough of our own stress, thank you very much."

"I concur," Carmen said, as she gathered her books.

"But the world is in trouble, crying out for us to help. We can't ignore that by obsessing over guys and clothes or what movie we should see on the weekend just so we don't have to look at the horrible reality we've created for ourselves," I rambled, clearly on a roll.

"Hey, it wasn't our generation that messed things up for us," Carmen said, snapping her locker shut. "And for the record, I vote for that spooky cruise ship movie opening Friday."

"Whatever, as long as it gets me out of the house," Ella chirped. "And just so you know, Sabine, it's not exactly cheery to hear the world is about to end. We're only sixteen and besides, we don't even drive yet and I'm pretty sure my

23   **earthgirl**

brother can drop us at the early show, but someone's units have to pick us up."

"It's not depressing," I answered, amazed but not at how they were trivializing something so important and somehow by extension also proving it so incredibly relevant. "I mean, it is a downer, but it doesn't have to be. It's also empowering. The only way to fix problems is to know what they are so you can do something."

"Good for you," Carmen smiled. "Go forth with your newfound fame and glory and be a fixer of the world and hopefully I can fix the C I got on my history test before the parentals find out and my almost-perfect universe falls apart, too. Cause that, girlfriend, would really, really suck large."

being here
why-a pariah?
[Sept. 27th | 09:41pm]
[mood | confounded]
[music | Hawksley Workman – Goodbye to Radio]

Despite the parental haranguing, I left the video up. For now. It's hardly the international show stopper I'd figured, getting nothing near the hits and visits it deserves (apparently becoming a YouTube phenom involves phenomenal amounts of energy, promotion and email contacts).

Still, what reaction i have had has been overwhelming.

Huge hugs and thank yous to the peeps offering support and encouragement.

A pox on you slaggers. Yeah sure, sticks and stones hurt more, but names sting too! It's weird. Am I the only one in my corner of the world who sees the validity of this new focus? Or am I delusional in thinking I can make a dent in the problem? In the complacency of my friends and their friends and so on, etc?

Yup. I guess I am. But I will do my very bestest to embrace the epic new challenge. I owe it to myself and the planet.

link   3 comments | post comment
www.savetheearth.org

onederful 09-29 11:22
Saw you fight the power! Good on ya! And don't be discouraged – there are 70 million video clips out there and it's hard to dis-tract people from bad karaoke and sleeping kittens. Sad but true. I'll fwd yer link to everyone I know! even the kitten lovers.

lacklusterlulu 19-29 23:53 (link) select
easy peasy get some new friends!

MachFhive 09-30 02:03
Yo bike freekz, if it had been me, Id have run you down. Splat.

"How much?" Carmen asked sweetly as she waved a lit-tle pink purse in front of a bored-looking street vendor set-ting up his table.

It was a sunny not-quite-crunchy fall Saturday after the

earthgirl

incident, and my girlz were hanging with me before my shift at a popular retail outlet that rhymes with nap. Somehow, at barely eleven a.m., we were downtown roaming Queen West for bargoons. Not that we exactly needed anything. It was just our ritual.

But today's version felt different for me. I felt different. It was like I was there but wasn't, watching the action like a spectator. And honestly, I didn't much like what I saw.

"For you, fabulous deal," the street vendor smiled. His right eyetooth was capped in gold. It flared in the sunlight.

"Well, I know that," Carmen cooed, blinking her eyelashes, "but you still didn't say how much."

"Twenty dollar each, three for fifty dollar," he said as Ella checked the zipper on a little yellow bag.

"Thanks, I don't want one," I announced.

BTI, or Before the Incident, I'd have gone for the deal. But standing there looking at the table full of trendy plastic purses, I lost my appetite for shopping. I lost my appetite for having something for the sake of just…having it. Zap, gone, just like my appetite for plum-goo-slathered chicken fingers after I found myself wearing them.

"But it's a pseudo Prada!" Carmen insisted, sniffing it and rubbing it across her cheek. "And even better, it's a steal."

"What do you need another fake bag for?"

"I prefer to call them tributes," Carmen said. "How much for two?"

"Two," the vendor said very slowly, like he was considering whether or not he'd donate his kidney. "For you, twenty dollars each. And these not fake. Real quality, top notch."

"That's not a deal!" Carmen pouted, putting down the pink purse abruptly and starting to walk away.

It was always like this. She loved haggling with the guys who sold things on the street. Especially pretty things she wanted to have, but didn't need. That all of us didn't remotely need, but would definitely be a better deal if we bought in bulk. For her it was a form of entertainment. And ours by default, I guess.

But at this particular moment it wasn't the least bit entertaining to me. It was actually a tad nauseating.

"Take three," the vendor insisted, holding out a lime green bag to me. "Is very beautiful. Very in."

I took the bag and unzipped it, then pulled out a wad of rough tissue stuffing and looked for a label to see where it had come from. How far this stylish thing had traveled to end up on this folding table in downtown Toronto being sold for a pittance.

"Where's it made?" I asked as Carmen pretended to look at the silver rings and trinkets on the next table.

"Italy," he grinned without missing a beat. "Is genwin Prada, see label?"

"They are very beautiful," Ella agreed. "And an excellent deal."

Carmen gave her a little hoof in the shin followed by a glare.

"What?" Ella moaned.

"They're not an excellent deal," Carmen hissed at her through clenched teeth. "But they could be."

"The person who made this probably got paid five cents an hour," I announced. "That's why they're so cheap."

"Not cheap." The vendor snatched the little bag from my hands. "Very top quality."

"Well, things probably don't cost as much where they are," Ella answered, running her hand softly over the stitching. "And you don't know, maybe five cents an hour is a lot of money there."

"You can't really believe that," I said. "That's less than a dollar a day. Nobody can live on that."

"You don't know how much they get paid, Sabine," Carmen chimed in. "Besides, I thought you were all hopped up about garbage. Since when did you start caring about someone making Prada knock-offs in China or Bolivia or whereveria? You work at the Gap."

"It's Gap, not the," Ella corrected. "Hey, can you get me one of those kicky orange hoodies on your discount before they sell out?"

"This is garbage. It's unnecessary, disposable crap," I replied, almost slamming my fist on the table. "Your life is fine without it."

"I'm aware of that, dummy. It's a little purse," Carmen said sensibly. "But that doesn't mean I want to live without it. Seriously, Sabine, you can't possibly think if we don't buy these they'll suddenly stop making them? Besides, then that poor worker in the Third World armpit won't even make a buck a day and their whole family will starve. Then how will you feel? Two for thirty, final offer."

Carmen held out thirty dollars to the vendor, who hesitated for a second before accepting it with a greedy grab.

"Have a nice day," the vendor beamed as he added the money to a honking wad of cash from his pant pocket.

"You, too," Ella sang, waving her shiny yellow bag at him.

"Don't be doing that again," Carmen warned as she leaned up against a fire hydrant and transferred the contents of her practically new tiny red purse into her extremely brand spanking new miniature pink one. "Swear off shopping if you want. It doesn't mean I have to."

"Don't you realize that just because something is a good deal for you, it might be a crap deal for someone else?" I said.

"So?" Ella asked as she modeled her little yellow shoulder bag in front of a store window. "Look how stylin' it is."

"So," I said, "maybe we should be thinking about things like that when we buy things, that's all."

"That's a relief," Carmen laughed. "I thought she was going to say, *IF* we buy things."

"Thinking about everyone else, huh?" Ella mused. "Nice idea, but I'll pass. Kinda takes all the fun out of it."

being here
consumer defiance!!!!!
[Sept. 29th | 06:39pm]
[mood | empowered!]
[music | green day – boulevard of broken dreams (apropos or what?!?!)]

SPONTANEOUS NON-CONSUMPTION: The impulsive instinct to NOT buy something. It's exhilarating and liberating! Seriously.

earthgirl

Think about it. Is fashion really worth enslaving someone on the other side of the world? Is tyranny and selfishness actually fashionable? Rhetorical question.

The point is let's just try to think more about NEED versus WANT. What we actually, truly, definitely require to function in this world and not just all the things the ads and commercials TELL US we want or SHOULD have. To be better, cooler, wiser, more complete!!!

Maybe the secret of being a good consumer is not being a consumer at all.

THE REVOLUTION WILL NOT INCLUDE A GIFT SHOP.

link   2 comments | post comment
www.storyofstuff.com
www.responsibleshopper.org

lacklusterlulu 09-29 22:22
Looks like you're a green bean now :) Welcome to the light side sister.
www.behindthelabel.org

three_

"You know that big natural food store beside Thompson's Hardware?" I asked Mom as she tore into a jumbo-sized box of garlic marinated chicken breasts. Like we were a family of fourteen rather than a garden-variety family of four.

I was fishing for her reaction to a place that didn't sell things in packages of a thousand so you could stock up for the next two hundred years every other weekend. Fishing to see if the sudden, subtle changes happening in me could influence or inspire any changes in her.

"I know if I'm ever in the market for chicken raised at a spa or thirty-dollar lettuce that's where I'd go," she answered.

"It's not thirty dollars for lettuce. And if the food is slightly more, that's because it's organic. Certified, even, chemical and pesticide free, which is better for your health."

"Oh," she nodded, looking up at me from the cutting board. "And this public service announcement wouldn't have anything to do with the little incident the other day, right?"

"Not exactly. Well, indirectly, maybe," I blurted. "And I start working there tomorrow."

31   **earthgirl**

To avoid her gaze I opened the fridge and snooped for something to munch. There were regular probably pesticide-soaked apples and processed cheese sticks in an unnatural shade of fluorescent orange. I settled on a kosher pickle.

"That's nice for you," she said, trying to not sound surprised but sounding incredibly surprised. "What happened to your other job?"

"I quit. They needed people at the Fresh Co-op and I thought it would be more interesting, maybe educational. And don't worry, I gave notice and all that."

"But they gave you such a great staff discount," she sighed.

"And I spent half my pay there on things I don't really need, while selling other people things they probably don't need," I answered as I crunched the pickle loudly to drown out her voice.

"So you don't need to wear clothes at the co-op? I didn't realize you'd turned into a nudist, too. Grab a few potatoes from under the sink," she pointed. "And if you're suddenly a vegetarian, see what's in the fridge that you approve of and get cooking. I'm not running a restaurant."

"Why are you making fun of me? All I did was get a new job. You should be encouraging me. I'm a good responsible daughter, you know."

"I know you are. I just didn't think your little encounter would, I don't know, change so much."

"You mean standing up for cleaner public spaces or waking up from the consumer coma we call life?"

"Don't be so melodramatic, Bean. You know I'm proud

that you stood up for yourself. Just don't blame me if I wish the entire world didn't see you having a scuffle with someone."

"And don't blame me. I didn't litter and I didn't video it or post it for that matter. I can't help it if I lived it, you know."

"You're right, honey," she said, washing her hands with antibacterial dish soap and wiping them dry on her jeans.

She stepped over to hug me and I stiffened. I was mad she wasn't happy that I was suddenly interested in the world. Moms are supposed to be supportive. At least to your face, anyway. If they have to make fun of you it's usually with your dad and behind your back. At least it should be.

"It's just one minute you're this fashion-obsessed teenager and I blink and you're a tree hugger," she sighed. "You can see where I might be a bit confused."

"I'm still me. I'm just trying to be a better me."

"I am proud of you," she smiled. "I really, truly am. And I'm sorry if I overreacted or was a little embarrassed. That's my thing and I shouldn't make it yours. Just like if something is your thing, you shouldn't make it ours."

"Even if—"

"You want respect, show a little back," she answered. "And please, promise me you won't stop showering. And if you decide to go live in the forest and I don't visit, it's only because I really hate bugs."

being here...still
UP A TREE WITHOUT A LADDER (or a paddle!!!)
[Oct 1st | 11:03pm]
[mood | optimistic]
[music | The Hideout - Sarah Harmer]

once upon a time, a brave girl with the coincidentally poetic
name JULIA BUTTERFLY HILL climbed a huge, ancient tree
in California to defend it from the anti-tree peeps salivating
to cut it down, their gnarly chainsaws revving – gerrrrrzzz.

did she stay a few days? weeks? nope. SHE STAYED FOR
TWO YEARS! she actually put down roots (ha!) in a tree
and for over SEVEN HUNDRED DAYS!!! IN A TREE!!!

now birds and squirrels live in trees but even they leave
once and a while to check out the 'hood or have a swim or
a date or gather food. not her. she lived in that tree like
she belonged there. like it was the most normal thing in the
world.

the people supporting her tree sit rigged a pulley to send
up food and water and books and letters of encouragement. they must have really loved and admired her since I
imagine they also had to pulley down her garbage and
laundry and yikes – poop! i mean really, what else did she
do with it?

i wonder if she was ever lonely or bored or afraid? i wun-
der if her mom ever brought sprout sandwiches?

PS: she saved the tree!! :)
link   3 comments | post
comment
www.circleoflifefoundation.org
www.ecotopia.org/ehof/hill

onederful 10-01 11:53
"We are constantly being told we are the
leaders of tomorrow, that's a lie. We are
the leaders of today." Julia Butterfly Hill.
Words to live by!
BTW yer new postings rock. And I love
rocks...and trees too!

altalake 10-01 23:58
Today, you are in a place to take the lead. No
pressure.

"So, you working here now?" the most gorgeous guy I'd
ever seen asked as he stood in front of me sniffing a fair
trade cantaloupe.

I'd hoped quitting the Gap gig and forfeiting my oh-so-
excellent merchandise deal to get a job at the health food co-
op would serve up karma points. And here was evidence
standing right in front of me. All six or so fabulous feet of it.

I nodded and smiled. I hoped I wouldn't fall over or
throw up.

"What happened to Josie?" he asked. "True she got busted for dealing meth?"

"I wouldn't know," I said softly, which was only half true.

I'd actually heard the girl I replaced was a tweaker who tried to deal out of the co-op, but didn't think it was my business to say. For all I knew this scorching hottie was one of her customers or even a baby-faced narc or worse maybe he was the big cheese supplier looking for a new kid to do his dirty work. I really hoped not. He was tall and fit and sonically cute and it would be a total drag if he turned out to be a big drug-dealing loser.

"It's probably not a bad thing," he said, putting the cantaloupe back neatly.

I had a strange urge to grab it and give it a nuzzle. Fruit had never looked sexier.

"She needed help," he shrugged, looking straight at me with his deep emerald green eyes. "That stuff is screwed-up poison and fries your brain."

"I've heard," I nodded, happy to discover he wasn't into that kind of stuff either. "Um, is there something I can help you with?"

He shook the thick black curls on his head and reached down into his orange courier bag. While he fished around and couldn't see me watching, I memorized him the best I could. That hair, those eyes, that blemish-free olive skin. The bulky hand-knit sweater that hugged him across his chest and belly. The khaki cargos with the fluorescent Velcro strap at his ankle, screaming serious bike rider. The canvas sneakers suggesting maybe he was a vegetarian (but hopefully not a vegan or raw foodie since that was way too far on the commitment continuum for me right now). The overwhelming yumminess that was this…this him!

I felt like a spy, except I was spying in plain view.

"My band is doing a benefit next week," he said, pulling a fistful of photocopies out of his bag. "For the Environmental Action League. I brought some flyers. And don't worry, recycled paper." He turned to the notice board and started moving a few things around to make space for his poster. He was very tidy and considerate about it.

"Sounds like a team of green superheroes," I said, thinking out loud and immediately regretting it. Regretting that I sounded like I was twelve and profoundly unhip in front of this profoundly, decidedly hip wonder of nature. How thoroughly humiliating.

"In some ways we are," hottie said, as if my comment actually wasn't stupid. "Keeping the world safe from corporate corruption and global idiocy before it's too late."

"Sounds brave and crucial," I said. "So what's your superpower?"

"For now I guess I'm No Logo Man," he answered, smiling and waving his hand in front of his sweater. "Keeping my mind and body free of commercial advertising. That is until my real superpower's revealed."

"Your real one?"

"It takes years sometimes. They..." he said, shifting his eyes back and forth, "want to make sure you're serious, committed to the cause. Know what I mean?"

I didn't have a clue, but I could listen to him talk for the rest of the year if he'd let me. I smiled and nodded as if it were obviously obvious.

"Nice to meet you, No Logo Man. I'm Sabine, superpower unknown so far," I said, biting my lower lip and lowering my eyes. I was feeling nervous and excited. I probably should have extended my hand, but by the time I realized, it was too late. And by then my hand was far too clammy.

"Nice to meet you, Sabine," he said, smiling and putting his hands together with little Buddha bow. "And it's Vray. I am."

"Hi, Ray."

"Not Ray. Vray."

"Excuse me?"

"Vray. It's like Ray with a V," he replied as he held up his hand in the V for victory peace sign gesture.

"With a V? I don't get it." I'd never heard that name before. I hoped I didn't sound ignorant or culturally insensitive.

"V-R-A-Y, I spell it with a Y. With an I, it means truth in French."

"Are you French?"

"Partly, but I prefer to think of myself as a citizen of the world."

"Me, too," I answered, thinking what a nice sentiment that was especially since Toronto-born and bred Canadian girl didn't exactly exemplify exotic. "Is that really your name?"

"Is Sabine really your name? It's not exactly the most common name either," he asked, leaning forward a bit. A bit more than I was prepared for at that particular second.

I thought I was going to hyperventilate, but happily it passed as I breathed in deeply through my nose. He smelled faintly like boy sweat and cinnamon toast. When I was in kindergarten, Jimmy Kerr used to smell like ketchup, but I'd never known a boy who smelled like cinnamon toast. It was strange and delicious. And a bit distracting.

"Hey, wasn't that bike girl in Kensington named Sabine, too?" he said suddenly, making little shadowboxing moves.

"Guess it's not an uncommon name then," I answered, unsure whether to brag or hide the truth, which wasn't exactly surprising since I was a bit unsure of how to keep from falling over at that moment.

"Funny that," he said, unclipping his bike helmet from the strap on his bag and hovering it up over my head like he was inspecting me.

"Yeah, coincidences, weird," I smiled as I guided the helmet toward my head, careful to not touch his fingers. Afraid of what might happen if I did.

"I don't believe in coincidences. It's just a handy word for things people aren't ready to admit mean something big."

"Funny that," I said quickly and just as quickly handing back his helmet like it was suddenly on fire or something. "So, um, Vray what? Do you have a last name or do you just go by Vray?"

I didn't care if I was being nosy. I had to get the subject back to him. It was too weird and uncomfortable for the subject to be me. Even if he seemed to be slightly interested. Scratch that, especially since he was.

"Foray."

"Vray Foray?" I knew there was more to it. To this yummy, socially conscious, warm and spicy-scented guy. A lot more.

"It's pronounced Foray, but it's spelled F-O-R-E-T. Most people get it wrong and it's boring to explain," he said, not seeming the least bit bored that he was explaining it.

"And do most people actually believe you were born with a name like forest of truth? What does it say on your student ID?" I knew I was probably being indelicate, especially since this was my feeble attempt at flirting, but this was getting more and more intriguing by the minute.

"People are named when they're a few days or a few hours old. It doesn't mean the people naming them get it right every time," he explained. "Who knows what agenda your parents had when they named you? Maybe someone won a coin toss or they were naming you after some old dead relative out of obligation, or a former lover or something equally stupid, so really it doesn't matter what it says on your birth certificate. That's who my parents decided I was when I sucked in my first breath. What matters is who I am now and what kind of person I plan to be in the future."

I stood there feeling like my mouth was open in awe. I rubbed my fingers on my chin and gave it a quick check and thankfully my lips were only slightly parted. But in a way, it was like someone had slapped me. Slapped me senseful. This totally gorgeous cinnamon bear of a guy with an ironic and rather idiotic name was a sage.

"Don't I get one of those?" I asked as he started stuffing the flyers back into his bag.

"Absolutely," he said, passing me one. "Bring your friends."

"I don't think they'd be into it," I said, once again catching myself thinking out loud.

"That's too bad. We're doing some important things, but then I don't have to tell you what you already know," Vray said.

"No," I said, the smile practically exploding off my face. "I mean, it's not my fault they're stuck in a rut, right? Maybe they'll come around. Anyway I'm cool with going places myself." I was happy I said that since I wasn't sure if it was actually true. I never really did things alone. Usually I hung out with Carmen and Ella or dragged my annoying sister along for company. And saying it made it sound like a promise.

"Good," he said, turning to leave. "I'll see ya, Sabine who may or may not have been scrapping on YouTube."

Oh, you'll see me, I thought. Elated at the idea that for once in my life someone and, more specifically, a boy someone, actually noticed me.

And maybe even wanted to see more of me. The new ever-improving me.

The real me.

four_

"Forest of truth? You've got to be fritchin' kidding. What kind of loser calls himself something like that? He's not an elf, is he?" Carmen was literally rolling on the carpet shaking with laughter. "Gotta give you credit, Sabine. At first I thought all your eco-crap stuff was just kind of pathetic. I didn't realize how full on entertaining it would be."

I immediately regretted telling her about Vray. About my new job at the co-op. About the concert. About anything. She may have understood most things about me, but that was before the whole wake-up-and-smell-the-flowers-before-they-aren't-around-to-smell wake-up call.

It was clear this was going to be harder to swallow. Carmen liked boys the way she liked most things. Predictable and malleable. I should have thought about that before I opened my mouth. To say I was totally smitten with a guy who had probably made up his own name.

"I knew you wouldn't be into the concert, but it's pretty cool what he's trying to do anyway," I said, tucking the neatly folded flyer under my social studies textbook.

"Are you whacked? And miss the granola groovefest of the year?" She sat up suddenly and propped herself against the foot of my bed. "And just to show how sincere I am, for solidarity, I won't even shave my legs, though I draw the line at pit fur, no matter how much you like him."

"You don't have to go. Really, it's fine," I said, realizing that going alone would be way better than being judged and mocked by my best friend. "It's not your thing, I totally know that. I only mentioned it because I didn't really have anything interesting to talk about."

"No, you mentioned it cause you're excited about maybe he's going to be my freaky new boyfriend and want moral support. Plus you need me to check him out. My psycho detector's much better than yours."

"That's because you've had more practice," I said as I crossed my arms over my chest.

"Don't get all huffy. I'm excited you met someone," she insisted. "I'd be more excited if he sounded less wiggy but whatever. We'll do our homework and decide if he's worthy or not."

Please, I thought, don't make that include some kind of disgusting balm or voodoo doll.

"If it's meant to happen, Carmen, it will."

"Right, now that you've moved into flake central the universe will provide everything so go hug a tree and save those seals and blah, blah, blah," she teased, even though she wasn't teasing. "I have to sleep on this to figure out the best strategy. I haven't seen you this amped about a guy since you chased Jimmy Kerr around his ninth birthday party."

"Thanks, but I don't want a strategy," I answered. "And he chased me."

"Fine, but let me know the second you want my help cause even if I'm not into your stupid shopping embargo, for this stuff I am so there for you."

"Great," I nodded, breathing deeply and wishing with all my heart that something would happen with Vray and me. Without Carmen meddling. Or anyone else.

That maybe I'd been the target of a minivan maniac for a reason. To incite my epiphany about the world being bigger than me and my friends, so I could stop being a spectator in my life and do something.

That it wasn't just a coincidence that Vray walked into the co-op the first hour of my very first day and talked to me, then quasi-recognized me and invited me to an environmental event even! That, like he said, there were no coincidences, just things we don't know the meaning of yet.

That he was going to make everything in the world possible. Even if that seemed crazy and impossible at this particular moment. That all this was part of the bigger plans for me now that I'd woken up from being some silly shallow girl.

Now that I was an earthgirl.

e a r t h g i r l
MY BODY IS NOT A BILLBOARD
[October 5th | 04:36pm]
[mood | crazed]
[music | Rage Against the Machine]

Today I realized that accidentally, inadvertedly I joined a club I never meant to join — THE CULT OF CON-

SUMERISM. But I am breaking out after reading NO LOGO, a book about the anti-globalization movement. written by a girl from my very own hometown of Toronto (Terrono, AKA t.dot) Canada.

Powerful. Insightful. Influential. Scarios. Check all of the above.

Fast forward to NoLogoMan (this hunk'o'hottie i just met) perhaps a true super hero fighting against global conglomoratization (if that's a word), unfair employment practices and sneaky stealth marketing babble everywhere.

Funny how most people in my universe will actually pay large to cover their bodies with logos and slogans. pay to advertise for companies in the mistaken belief this elevates their status. NOT ME.

I WILL NOT BE A WALKING HUMAN BILLBOARD.

Wow, it's going to take work to sort through all this, but i'm definitely going to think about these things more so I can do something about them. later...bean!

link   read 5 | post
www.getethical.com
www.nologo.org

earthbound01 10-05 18:40
Bean is my sister's nickname. So by extension I think that everyone named Bean must be cool. I also have a copy of No Logo, but I

earthgirl

haven't read it yet. Also, Toronto is one of the coolest cities I've ever been to.

altalake 10-05 23:58
I read in an interview that when Naomi Klein who wrote that book was 17, she was designer mad (as in crazed) before she got globally conscious. So don't be too hard on yourself earthgirl. It all starts somewhere.
www.corpwatch.org

"You forgot to flush again," Clare shouted from my bedroom doorway, the distinctive drone of Sum 41 leaking out of her oversized DJ headphones.

"That so better not be my iPod," I answered.

"What?" she yelled at a volume that was extreme even for her.

As per usual, she was all jocked out in her latest yoga-slash-running-slash-kickboxing outfit. No doubt fantasizing about some international competition despite her sorry lack of athleticism.

"Ask next time you borrow something," I groaned, pointlessly putting out my hand for the iPod.

"What's that got to do with making me see your stuff in the toilet?" she asked as she slipped the cans off her ears, barged in and glared over my shoulder at my homework. Which was actually not exactly homework, but a bunch of potentially embarrassing doodles of Vray's and my name that I quickly covered from her nosy eyeballs.

"If it's yellow let it mellow. If it's brown flush it down," I said, trying to shoo her back by extending my foot in a mock stretch.

"That's so completely gross," she whined.

"No it's not. Every time you flush the toilet, seventeen liters go down the drain."

"Yeah? So what's your point?" she snorted as she put her hands on her hips and cracked her gum.

"That it's not mandatory to flush every time you take a wee," I sighed, already exhausted by her since it could hardly be more obvious. And she could hardly be more exhausting.

"Who died and made you queen of the bathroom?" she asked as she expertly picked her way through my make-up collection on the dresser before settling (of course) on my very fave, now-discontinued lip color.

I leaned forward and grabbed it out of her hand. She cracked her gum again louder. It made me want to rip it out of her mouth.

"In Singapore it's illegal to chew gum unless you have a medical exemption," I said. "And anyone found dealing gum can be sentenced to up to two years in prison."

"You're completely crazy," Clare answered. "First of all this is Canada and second of all, I'm so telling Mom." She flicked her ponytail and swiveled in her sparkly runners toward the door.

"Ireland taxes it to help pay for the mess it makes on streets," I yelled through the slamming door.

Chew on that for a while.

Brat.

e a r t h g i r l
all plastic is not fantastic
[October 7th | 08:33pm]
[mood | bewildered]
[music | Cat Power — The Greatest]

Though it's impossible to imagine a world without plastic
[heck, I'm typing this on a plastic keyboard, guided by a
plastic mouse, sending it down plastic coated cables into
the rest of the plastic universe] might it not be possible to
give up on the humble yet not so humble plastic grocery
bag?

In Ontario, 2.5 billion plastic bags are sent to landfill each
year! Plastic bags made of natural gas and oil, that take
400 years to biodegrade and leach into water, etc.

I'm not a total fool or hypocrite here. I know we need plastic. But I also know we don't need plastic bags. Proof? In
Ireland they put a 25 cent tax on them and consumption
dropped by 90%. I may move to Ireland. The isle of green.
Land of the leprechaun. Land of less ucky gum and plastic
detritus!

link   read 5 | post
www.planetark.com

altalake 10-07 11:58
At the age of 6 months, the average Canadian
has consumed the same amount of resources as an
average person in the developing world. There

are 6.5 billion people in the world.
www.census.gov/ipc/www/world.html

onederful 10-08 00:13
In Mumbai, pollution from plastic bags is
so bad, it clogs the sewer system and causes flooding. Over 700 tonnes of garbage is
dumped each day and 20% is plastic bags. In
China, used Styrofoam packaging is called
white pollution. And 16% of Russia is so
toxic, it's uninhabitable. It also has a
name: ECOCIDE.

earthgirl
[October 08th | 07:33am]
Wow! Thanks for sharing those scary stats guys!
Seriously. :) And thanks especially for taking me seriously.
Seriously.

five_

The Environmental Action League benefit was the following Sunday afternoon. I was totally choked to see I'd been skedded to work at the exact time the concert would be going off. Since I was only a few shifts into my new job, I was terrified to ask Tom the co-op manager to move things around.

So much for my recently amassed karma points. This was a big fat cosmic wrench. I only wished I hadn't promised the delicious Vray Foret I'd be there and maybe played harder to get. Or at least acted indifferently interested and not superdooper keen interested. Now Vray would think I was unreliable, a poseur and a liar. That is, if he ever bothered to think about me again.

I must have been staring at the poster like a lovestruck zombie or something when I sensed someone behind me.

"The Monkey Wrench Gang bite." It was Ruby, this totally awesome eco-conscious art college girl who had worked at the co-op on and off since high school. "But their hearts are in the right places so that counts for something, I guess."

"It keeps them living and breathing," I sighed. "Guess you're going, right?"

"I'd rather have your shift if you want to go," she said calmly.

"Really?"

"Sure," she smiled back. "I can always use the extra hours and from what Tom says, you're here to expand your world view and not being here next weekend is the ideal way."

"I really appreciate it," I gushed.

"No biggie. I'm happy to do it," she said as she turned to go back to work.

Amazing. She barely knew me, yet she was still so kind and cooperative. Then again, this was a co-op, so maybe it just went with the territory. What a strange and exciting new world.

• • •

The plan was for Carmen and Ella to meet me at Lee's Palace, this club on Bloor Street in the University of Toronto neighborhood called the Annex. The flyer said the concert started at four. I figured that was since it was an all-ages show and probably the only time the club, which was an actual bar, was available.

There were two bands listed, but I'd forgotten to ask Vray if he was in the Ruby-panned Monkey Wrench Gang or O-Zone. I hoped he was in O-Zone. And since I didn't know who was on first and didn't want to risk missing a nanosecond of Vray on stage, or anywhere, I decided to be punctual. Also, who knew if the benefit would sell out and I'd be stuck without a ticket.

Not wanting to appear too keen or geeky, I stalled on the sidewalk for ten minutes scanning the mishmash of posters stapled, taped and pasted on the hydro poles. There were sure a lot of cheap movers, yoga/Pilates classes and vintage movies around.

Finally, when it seemed like it would be okay to go in, I did. This waifish girl with big thick knotted dreadlocks in a Mohawk stamped a turtle on my fist in exchange for my five dollars.

Aside from a couple of musician-looking guys and two girls at a table with a homemade banner with a cartoon of the earth, the joint was empty. I wasn't sure if I should go back out and wait for the girls or wander in, but since I was this far and my shoes were practically stuck to the goopy floor, I ventured toward the info table.

The bar smelled like stale beer and feet. And it was incredibly dark and unattractive. No wonder people drank in places like this.

I had just picked up a pamphlet on global warming when I felt a hand on my shoulder.

"You made it," Vray said as I spun around, nearly knocking him over.

"I said I would," I answered, hoping he might step close enough that his cinnamon scent would kill the stench of old socks.

"Pretty shite turnout." He gestured toward the empty room. "Can't believe how apathetic people are about doing the right thing."

"It's still early," I said, even though I was totally clueless about whether anyone else was coming. If even my best chiquitas would be there or would bail when they caught a whiff of the kinda lame action.

"True, and the people who don't show will be sorry they missed out," he said. "Years from now they'll all be claiming they were at the historic gig of two seminal bands."

"So who plays first?" I asked.

"O-Zone, that's my band. Well it's not really mine exactly since ownership is such a bourgeois concept, but I founded it."

"Cool," I said, because I didn't know what else to say and it seemed like I should say something.

"It's from the Greek for smell," he explained, and I couldn't help thinking how appropriate that was, considering I had my nose plugged as best I could. And also wishing I had a dictionary handy to look up any new words Vray might toss my way.

"Monkey Wrench Gang is a cute name for a band," I gushed, immediately wishing I had something more impressive to say.

"It's hardly cute. They're named for a rad collective of eco-warriors, earth liberators and forest saviors."

"Like Julia Butterfly Hill?" I asked, thrilled that I actually now knew something about people on the frontlines of the tree movement.

"The chick who lived in the tree?"

"Yeah," I nodded. "Poetic, don't you think?"

"If you consider having a Simpson's episode based on you cool. Not that I wouldn't be down with a tribute like that. It's just not why I'm into the cause, you know," he said, though I absolutely didn't know. "I'm not exactly into the touchy-feely thing as the kind of action that will save the world."

"So what would you do instead?" I asked, genuinely curious and imagining loud protests full of cargo-pant-wearing bandana-masked hoodlums dodging tear gas and police on horses (something that seemed equal parts thrilling and terrifying).

"Well," he sighed, looking at me with his big green eyes, "the band is one thing, for sure. Music is a good way to get the message out there. I mean, look at Zack de la Rocha or that Bono dude. But I have a few other tricks up my sleeve. Stuff that definitely gets noticed and will make a difference in how people act in the future."

I was dying to hear more, but just then I spotted Carmen and Ella across the room. Carmen had on her holier-than-thou scowl, which I guess wasn't really surprising. This was definitely not her scene, even if she was a good enough friend to suck it up and pretend it might be fun before she and Darren hooked up for the night. Ella had her usual sweet oblivious grin plastered across her face.

Carmen caught my eye and they bolted from the information table like it might be toxic and scooted over.

"This is Vray and this is Ella and Carmen," I said, realizing what an odd mix we were. Vray all ratty and secondhand and my two best gals in designer duds.

"We've heard a lot about you," Carmen said, her eyelashes batting like plastic spiders.

I wanted to elbow her in the side for being so obvious and embarrassing, but fortunately Vray didn't react to her comment unless you count his awesome smile getting bigger and more awesome.

There was an awkward hour-like moment while we all stood there sussing each other out and waiting for someone to say something.

Carmen broke the silence. "Darren's coming with Corey Crawford."

"That's great," I smiled, relieved there might be a few more people in the place, even if they were far from my fave people.

Then we half nodded our heads at each other in silence for one of those seconds that lasts six years.

"Well, I'd stay and chat, but I've gotta book, so thanks for coming and inviting people," Vray said, breaking the lull as he boxed me softly on the shoulder. "Sabine, you're definitely an asset to the cause." And with that he turned and headed off toward the stage.

"That was so incredibly weird," Carmen said.

"I know, that endless silence was pretty embarrassing," I agreed, not sure whether to ask if they thought he was flirting as much as I hoped.

"Not that. The whole 'asset to the cause' crap," she scoffed. "Your massive YouTube debut flopped. How is that an asset to anything?"

Carmen's words felt like kicks in the gut, but I took a deep breath. It wasn't my fault the sleeping kittens won out over my almost fisticuffs with a lunatic.

"He's excited she's here. She's practically a local legend," Ella jumped in, gushing. "Plus, she brought us to brighten the place up."

"Yeah, well he should be," Carmen agreed, looking

around at what couldn't even be called a thin crowd. In fact the word crowd barely figured into the equation at all.

"I think he's supremely yummy," Ella said. "I'm not sure about the nose ring or grotty jeans, but maybe that's his trademark rockstar thing."

I watched as Vray sat at the edge of the stage tinkering with a beat-up electric guitar in his lap and thought about how lucky I was that he'd walked into my life. If he hadn't, I'd be at the co-op stocking whole grain cereal.

Instead I was at this potentially cool concert for a cause, though what that cause was I wasn't exactly sure beyond the mysterious Environmental Action League moniker. And, I'd met serious guy with serious potential.

For the first time in my entire life I was getting to know a boy who was artistic and intense. Hunky yet concerned about the world, and not just if the Leafs would ever win the Stanley Cup again, or if he'd have his parents' car on the weekend. Someone I had things in common with. Real things, not stupid school things like if Mr. Butler would ever get the message about the breath mints people left on his desk, or if poor Corey Crawford would ever not be boring.

I was in bad. And I was in deep. And it felt absolutely exhilarating!

• • •

A few songs into O-Zone's set, there were about two dozen people in the still essentially empty bar. I tried to ignore the lack of support and instead concentrated on Vray. He thrashed at his guitar and bounced around the stage screaming stuff about smog and sediments (or maybe he was saying sentiment). His voice was raspy and a little tuneless, but what he lacked in actual talent, he definitely made up for in enthusiasm and energy.

"This is so lame," Carmen sniffed over the rangy guitars. "And there's no one here. I'm telling Darren to bail."

She dug into her perky pink plastic purse for her equally perky and pink cellphone.

"Shane McCardle is here," Ella giggled with a baby wave in his direction.

"So? He's a stoner," Carmen answered, flipping open the phone.

"Is not. He just has stoner hair and clothes."

"Yeah," Carmen nodded, dragging out the word for extreme emphasis and widening her eyes. "Cause he's a stoner."

"I feel horrible for Vray," I shouted. "He worked so hard to make this happen and no one cares enough about the earth to even show up."

"Maybe that's because his band sucks," Carmen shrugged as she deftly punched a text message with her long manicured nails. As if Carmen were suddenly the authority on all that was hip and sonically sound (admittedly, they weren't the best band I've ever seen, not that I've seen a ton of bands).

"You can go if you want," I said, even though I didn't really mean it.

"Thanks, Beanie, you rock," Carmen said, giving me a hug. "And way more than O-Zone." And with that she

57 **earthgirl**

made the devil horns with her fist as she and Ella turned and headed toward the back of the empty black hole. Making it feel even more empty and a little sad.

• • •

"I liked the song about toads," I told Vray as he gulped back water from a dented and stickered SIGG bottle.

"Thanks," he nodded, running his sleeve across his mouth and making me wish I were his sleeve. He sounded distracted and a bit exhausted. I guess I would be, too, if I'd had a benefit and barely anyone showed up.

I hoped that having a new convert like me offered a bit of consolation. Even if my being there was equal parts interest in the earth and in him.

"You were better than the Monkey Wrench Gang, in my humble opinion, anyway," I added, wishing I knew Vray well enough to give him a hug to make him feel better for the show totally biting. And to make me feel better, too. It was hardly the explosive experience I wanted for my debut earthgirl activity. But mostly I was disappointed for him.

"Look, Sabine, it's cool you came out, but Finn and me gotta get the amps back to the rental place. Then I have to study for calculus," he explained.

"Sure," I nodded, blindsided by the abrupt end. But then he scribbled his coordinates on the back of a cardboard drink coaster.

It's funny how when I sniffed it after he left, I didn't seem to mind the smell of sweat and stale beer.

e a r t h g i r l
Car(e)-free Me...
[*Oct. 12th* | *09:53pm*]
[mood | enthralled]
[music | hallelujah by leonard cohen the rufus wainwright
version]

Apparently, in addition to the EAL concert, today was also
carfree Sunday. A carnival of non-car-related frolic.

People were dancing and doing yoga on the road! I even
saw some people having a picnic, blanket and all, by the
curb! The girl pouring tea even put money in the parking
machine and had the little paper receiptflapping fr om the
bell of her bike.

Crazy adorable. Except for the honking and cussing drivers in the zombie army who wanted her space for their
monster machines. Space she'd paid for and was just as
entitled to as them.

Public space. Everybody's space.

link   read 3 | post

Vague-a-bond 10-12 21:01
sounds like that action league benefit may have had benefits.
wink^2, nudge^2.
coming soon, some fr-eco action!

e a r t h g i r l
[Oct. 13th | 07:38am]
Dearest V, even though I don't know you beyond this special *everybody* space, I'm so happy to know you. Thanks
for your kindness and encouragement.

Vague-a-bond 10-13 10:13
aw shucks, grrlfriend. backatcha

Hey Vray. No, that sounds silly. *Yo Vray*. Not. Maybe just
a plain old *hi*. But then what? *Thanks for inviting me to the
show.* Too lame. Maybe *Hey, I was totally amped to be at your
awesome gig and super choked other people opted out.* Wrong!

Whatever I wrote had to be profound and perfect
because (a) that's what and who I wanted to be and (b) Vray
seemed like a profound kind of person. Like someone who
held onto things that were meaningful. And for all I knew,
he might be forwarding my emails to Finn or any of his
other eco-associates or bandmates. Nah, most guys probably
didn't do that, and he seemed too private, but still if I e-ed
him it would have to be stellar. Beyond stellar, if that was
even possible.

I guess I could always phone. And say what? *How was
your calculus test? Did you get the rental gear back in time?*

Ahhhhhhh! This was infuriating. Especially since
Carmen's boy-catching expertise could be incredibly helpful
at times like this and yet there was absolutely no way in hell
I'd enlist her now. Not after her snarky post concert TXT.

***Hot-T YES! Also mopey misguided potentially unstable.
Seriously ???-able BF material :(***

I didn't even give her the dignity of responding. I mean
it's not like I forced her to go, or invite then uninvite her
own boyfriend, and I never promised it would be interesting. There was absolutely no need to be rude and judgmental and insensitive to both of us. Not that there was an *us*
exactly, not precisely yet, anyway.

"Hey, Bean, what's going on?" my dad asked as he shyly
poked his head into my room.

"Nothing," I answered, slamming my laptop shut.

"You're not surfing for dirty pictures, I hope," he
laughed. "Or worse, shopping."

Dads were so embarrassing when they tried to be funny.
I gave him my best what-do-you-want-and-why-are-you-
bugging-me-in-my-sacred-space glare. Unfortunately, it
didn't work and he wormed his way into my room and sat
on the edge of my bed. He picked up my Pokemon pillow
(revered for its status as the first and only prize I ever won
at the Ex) and started punching it in the face.

"Do you mind?"

"Right, sorry," he nodded, putting it back amidst my
plushy and pillow collection, which suddenly seemed very
little girlie. "Pokemons are people, too. Anyway, I see you're
busy with that web diary or whatever it is you do all day and
night when you probably should be doing homework. I
wanted to give you this." He reached behind his back and
passed me a plastic bag from Indigo, this giant megabook-

store chain. I think he'd tucked it into the waist of his chinos.

"Try blogging, streaming, Facebooking or checking MySpace," I corrected as I peeked inside the bag and pulled out the crunchy new book – *The Complete Idiot's Guide to Global Warming*.

"Since you're getting into the earth-mother-nature-girl thing, I picked it up for you," he smiled proudly. Like I might have decided to be a dentist like him or could suddenly speak a dozen languages fluently including Elvish.

I thumbed through it, then gave him my most evil gaze.

"I'm not an idiot," I huffed and threw the book at him. I cringed as it bounced off Chichi, my stuffed lion, and landed on the duvet half open, its cover now crumpled.

"No one said you were," he answered, looking very startled and ironing the big fold in the cover with his palm. "It's just a book. It's just what they call it, that's all."

"Then why do you and Mom keep making fun of me?" I asked, completely pissed off he'd proven my theory that parents had nothing better to do than talk about you behind your back and worse, mock you! And more than that also had an annoying knack for interrupting you when you were dealing with the profound implications of contacting the guy you were madly crushing.

"I thought you might like it, that's all," he said, sounding genuinely hurt. "I can take it back."

"No," I said, because the truth was it actually looked like it could be informative, even if it had such a stupid title. "Thanks for getting it, but next time you get me a book you should support the small independent stores. Ruby from work says we have to or they'll disappear."

"Okay," he said giving my hair a ruffle like I was a dog or a baby. "Whatever you say, my little activist."

And with that he ducked out of my room.

Parents are so utterly lame.

six_

"See how this painting has a blue sky background and this one is gray and hazy?" Vray said, pointing to a dark oil painting of some decrepit old buildings and bridges. "That one dates before the Industrial Revolution. That's why the sky is bright. This one was painted after, when there was smog in the air all the time."

And here I'd been thinking I'd be lucky if our inaugural face-to-face was at some indie-coffee-shop-type venue. Instead we were wandering through the Art Gallery of Ontario talking about what art revealed about our world. Could there be a more perfect way to expand my burgeoning social consciousness, my artistic sensibilities and world view?

"Come on, that can't be true," I said, thinking this was all too strange to be possible. That we were discussing politics, the environment and history and it was almost sexy. Plus the fact that even over a hundred years ago, people were apparently as indifferent to pollution as they were now. No wonder things were such a stinky mess.

"We're talking about the 1850s. Photography had been invented, but was in its early stages and pretty experimental and expensive, so paintings were the main way people documented the world."

"But why was there so much pollution? I thought cars were one of the biggest problems," I said, marveling at how clever and informed and insightful Vray was for being only seventeen. And marveling even more at how I could be standing in front of these significant documents of history while the world's history of stupidity and destruction repeated itself.

"They're an issue, but back then people burned coal, one of the dirtiest forms of energy, for almost everything. Manufacturing, heating, cooking. And it made everything gray. Not that we learned anything, since we still burn tons of it every day, instead of demanding cleaner energy."

We wandered past more ominous paintings of pudgy, pink-faced people in dark, gloomy settings.

"Smog is just a combination of smoke and fog. When the smoke rose into the atmosphere and met with the fog that's so common in Britain, it got stuck there, so you ended up with smog."

"How do you know all this?" I asked, amazed that he obviously read so much stuff outside of school. And especially that he cared enough to get informed. So much for grown-ups whimpering about teen indifference. Vray was a living, breathing example of a social-conscious keener.

"I used to watch Jeopardy a lot." He smiled that seriously swoon-inducing smile.

"Seriously," I asked, giving his biceps (his apparently very muscular biceps!) a little squeeze. I realized with a pleasant shudder that it was the first time I'd actually touched him. Wow. You could fall in love in an art gallery, I thought, wondering if it might be happening right now.

"Books, talking to people. My mom and dad teach at U of T, and their blowhard friends always argue and debate this and that. Mostly useless academic stuff and I want to do more than just talk about ideas."

"It's like our parents and their generation made a complete mess of everything and it's up to us to fix it."

"It's debatable how much can be fixed," Vray said flatly. "So much stuff is beyond the point of no return. The only thing we can do is maybe slow down the inevitable decline of civilization and send out some pretty loud warnings about the consequences."

"That's awful," I said, wondering if we really were on our way to the end of the earth in a speeding car with no brakes (and who exactly was driving). "If we can't make a difference, what's the point of your environmental action-hero thing? Or the band? Or anything, for that matter?"

"It's seriously cute how worked up you get about all this," Vray said as he looked at me.

"I'm not trying to be cute," I said, even though I was exquisitely thrilled that he thought I was. "I'm just trying to do something and now you're telling me there's no point. You do realize the doomsday stuff is kind of a downer?"

As the words left my mouth, I seriously hoped I didn't sound like Carmen and Ella, since that was a million miles from what I intended. I was just baffled he could be so informed and so defeatist in the same breath.

"Everything we do to acknowledge the mess and strain on the planet helps. It sets an example," he explained, wrapping his fabulous strong arm around my shoulder and pulling me in for a demi-hug as we walked through the gallery. "But it doesn't change the cycle of humanity, which obviously points to our eventual extinction. It happened before. It'll happen again. Trick is to be the best you can be and keep the world as pristine as you can while you're here."

His arm had dropped from its contact with my body, but I could still feel the warmth where he'd touched me. I'd probably have melted then and there if we hadn't paused in front of a blue and white iceberg painting by Lawren Harris, my favorite Group of Seven artist. Even though his style was globby and cartoonish, you could almost feel the cool breeze coming off the barren northern landscape. The now-disappearing North of frozen glaciers, icebergs, ice floes and apparently not-so-permanent permafrost.

The moment was so epic, so profound, I was frantic to say something to mark it. Something significant and meaningful and decidedly uncute.

Then I remembered a little blurb I'd found flipping through the Idiot's Guide (which actually turned out to be pretty informative and interesting. Thanks, Daddy!).

"In thirty years Glacier National Park won't have any more glaciers," I said as we stared intensely at the painting of snow and ice.

"Then we don't have a lot of time, do we," he said, taking my hand (my happily for once unclammy hand) and leading me through the maze of exquisite paintings.

I wasn't sure if he meant us or the world. Or maybe they were the same thing.

e a r t h g i r l
space invaders
[Oct. 14th | 11:53pm]
[mood | besotted, bewitched and bewildered]
[music | beth orton – galaxy of emptiness]

Sacred spaces. It seems like a simple concept, except every single day the corrupt corporate conglomorization of the world eeks and sneaks a bit more territory.

Take the Nevada desert, which the KFC people just did!! They put a gianormous mosaic of Colonel Freaking Saunders there which can be seen from outer space!

The aliens are going to think we all have white goaties and Buddy Holly glasses. It's so, so, so incredibly sad.

link   read 7 | post
googleearth

onederful 10-15 17:04
who is buddy holly?

Vague-a-bond 10-15 17:23
some dead musician guy who had the same glasses as Uncle KFC.

```
altalake 10-16 1:12
Clever tactic — colonel(izing) outer space via
the UFO capital(ists) of the world. Expanding
market share everywhere.
```

My occasionally adorable, often annoying little sister has
been recruited by the enemy. Like many thousands of other
easily impressed and impressionable girls before her and
sadly likely to follow, the POWERS THAT BE have co-
opted her mind in the name of uberconsumerism.

Yes, Clare was now a card-carrying, log-in accessing
member of the Girls Intelligence Agency.

It's enough to make me want to scream. I tried to inter-
vene. But sadly, as with my equally malleable, consumer-
corroborating and completely consumed dearest pals, it was
to little avail. Clare now gleefully reports to THEM, the
corporate behemoths (big mouths) with the satisfied oblivi-
ousness of a cult member. All because they have created this
groovy website, call her a secret agent and promise her free
stuff for a few strategic clicks.

This extremely clever subterfuge is designed to make her
believe she's actually an agent of change, influencing corporate decision making and consequently creating better
things for everyone everywhere. Provided your definition of
"everyone" is limited to middle-class girls in the Western
world. Like they needed to do more to get *everyone* on the
planet buying and wanting and consuming more!

Yes, being part of GIA (very glam sounding) means making
the world a better place for you and me and girls just like us.

"Don't you get it? They're making you think you're part of some special club and your opinion actually matters," I explained when she logged into the website to show me how "kewl" it was.

"Yeah, so?" She didn't even look at me as her fingers flew across the keyboard.

"So they're exploiting you," I said as I realized how incredibly brilliant and subversive this new under-the-radar advertising actually was. And how scary.

"No, they give me free stuff," she answered, expertly clicking the mouse onto the sleepover kit section.

"They trade it for your opinions so they can figure out what else they can sell you."

"So?"

"So? If you're a guinea pig and they're sucking your brain out, it's not exactly free."

"You really need to relax, Sabine. Try to get some groping action or something," she scoffed, turning toward me long enough to roll her eyes. "You're like some eco-crazy crazy person."

"No, I'm more like the only sane person I know," I sighed.

I wanted to be a good influence. I was trying to lead by example. But how could I possibly compete with free stuff?

Apparently being the earthgirl, and actually making a difference in my world, was going to require greater ingenuity on my part. And that was something I definitely know cannot be bought.

Anywhere. For any price.

e a r t h g i r l
[*Oct. 20th* | *9:58pm*]
[mood | confused]
[music | I was a daughter | Basia Bulat]

today i beg and implore you to just say no to fast food.
and not merely cuz of conglomeration + healthy eating concerns. for the garbage! gazillions of Styrofoam clamshells
for 5 minutes of transport lying in our ocean-sized landfills
for decades.

but since i'm not so naive to think the world will stop eating
fast food or taking out takeout, i came up with a most brilliant eco-innovation to solve this quandary. edible packaging! and then, to my pleasure, i discovered that it sort of
exists. some fabo folks are using corn and potatoes and
starch to make takeaway boxes that biodegrade and won't
be doomed to the ground for all eternity.

pretty clever! and kind. so if you must takeaway, then
demand more from the businesses you patronize!

theearthgirl@rocketmail.com

link   read 5 | post
www.naturopack.org
www.nat-ur.com
www.earthshell.com

altalake 10-20 21:21
I always carry my spork and Swiss army knife

and even have a plastic container in my pack.
Waste not, want not.

Vague-a-bond 10-21 00:22
Me, I like slow food and raw food and always, always, always,
local food.

seven_

Vray was sitting with his bandmate buddy Finn in the window seat of the midtown fair-trade all-organic coffee shop he'd suggested as our rendezvous point. I tried not to be too disappointed that he wasn't alone. Maybe I'd misinterpreted his text message and wished it into a date-date when it was just a casual hanging-out kind of thing.

From the sidewalk it looked like they were in the midst of an intense life-and-death discussion. I was almost reluctant to interrupt for fear I might derail what was certain to be an important train of profound thoughts.

I was considering the best mode of approach when Vray spotted me and waved me over. His serious expression suddenly shifted to the seductive smile, saving me from myself again, and not a second too soon.

"They're hypocrites of the highest order. It's beyond disgusting and obviously criminal," Finn ranted as I approached.

"Sounds intense," I offered, because his breathless indictment of whomever he was breathlessly indicting sounded so passionate and convincing. I didn't even know the topic, but already I was on side.

"Bastards are going to rip up the Arctic National Wildlife

Refuge to drill for oil," Finn sighed as he dragged a stool over to let me scooch in between them. So thoughtful and polite, considering his mind was elsewhere on something obviously big and calamitous.

"They have these rules to protect places and things, but they mean shit when money comes into the picture. It's unbelievable. The American asshole government gives its stamp of approval and everyone nods and agrees it's a good idea. Then they trot out the scientists they pay off to dispute the real science," Vray practically spat, the vein in his temple pulsing. "A whole species of caribou is threatened and instead of trying to develop clean renewable energy, it's *Hey let's drill for oil over here in case we can't have any more from the Mid East and we can't admit that illegal immoral war we launched isn't working out so well.* Damn all the animals and the landscape."

"But if it's a National Wildlife Refuge, doesn't that mean it's protected?" I asked, feeling confused and suddenly angry that I had no idea this was happening on top of all the other awful things going on in the world. When you took a second to think about it, all the everythings we didn't know were pretty frightening.

"Protected until big money pays off a few strategic powerbrokers," Vray answered with a sigh. "It's like why piss off the car makers and big oil? As if they're more important than creatures that were here way before us." He looked exhausted and a bit defeated. Not unlike the way he looked after his benefit concert bit the biscuit.

"So what do you do? I mean, what do we do?" I asked,

feeling small and powerless. The same way the poor soon-to-be-destroyed Arctic caribou would be feeling, if they knew what was going on. "Maybe you could have another concert outside somewhere to attract a bigger crowd."

"Yeah," Vray nodded. "We're thinking about a few bigger more intense things. The shows are good, but they don't get people riled up the way they should. We're still figuring it out."

"Let me know what I can do. I'll definitely help out," I said, even though I had no idea what I was offering. It's just that seeing him so emotional and committed made me feel like it was the least I could do. After all, I lived on this planet, too, and I hoped it would be around for many more years. For me and all the other people inhabiting it and the caribou (cariboos?), too.

"You're awesome, Sabine Solomon. Like I told Finn, I could tell the minute I saw you there was something real special going on," Vray said as he leaned forward and kissed me deftly and casually full on the mouth.

FULL ON THE MOUTH!!!

"Welcome aboard," Finn agreed, shaking my hand with a hip-hop handshake and acting like nothing monumentous had just happened.

To me! With his friend Vray! Right in front of his own nose! Like something called a KISS! By this point I was too stunned to actually hear what they said to one another.

It was fluky, fabulous moments like this that kind of made me wish I had an audience or a fan club, or that I could text with my mind to let Carmen and Ella in on what had just transpired. They didn't have a clue what an incred-

75

ible integrity-filled passionate guy Vray was. And that said amazing, valiant creature was really and truly interested in my ideas and contributions and, it now seemed, my company and my mind and my bod, too!

"It's made with rice milk. Better for you and the planet," Vray said as a steaming bowl of café au lait magically appeared on the beaten-up and graffiti-ed table in front of me.

I nodded and smiled. I was so lost in the extreme fabulosity of that surprise kiss that I didn't even remember him asking what I'd wanted. Or even noticing that Finn seemed to be gathering up his stuff.

"Gotta book," Finn said as he stood and shrugged on his heavy canvas jacket. "Later, bro. You, too, Sabine."

"Bye," I sighed and half waved as he headed out the door and the bell above it chirped sweetly.

"So was work okay?" Vray asked.

"Yeah, it's always different. We're selling a new line of vegan gluten-free eggless crackers, so I was giving out samples."

"They any good?"

"Not really. They're kind of dry, like little slabs of cardboard with sesame seeds. Not that I've ever eaten cardboard, but for some reason other people like them. Don't hate me for saying it, but some of that stuff is an acquired taste."

"I hear you," he said. "It gets easier with practice or if you're really, really hungry."

He smiled that melt-inducing smile again. I tried to stay calm and normal, since I didn't want him to think I was a total freak. Even though I felt like a total freak for wigging out over something other girls would consider so normal.

"So were you and Finn hanging out or was that official action hero business?" I asked.

"Both. Sorry if I ambushed you having him here. It was kind of last minute. He's a busy dude so even though I'm usually slammed, my time's more flexible."

"Don't you work at all?" I asked, genuinely intrigued that Vray was somehow so busy and available at the same time.

"No time with school, the band, the movement," he shrugged.

"What about money?"

"For what? I live at home, my mom feeds me, school's still free. I get by," he smiled, running his hand through his tangle of curls.

"Lattes, for example?" I pointed to the big bowl in front of us.

"Sarita comps me from time to time," he said, nodding to a plump, pretty, intense-looking girl with a brow ring wiping the espresso machine.

"What if you want to buy something?" I asked, wondering how he managed to have no job and no money problems, while I had a part-time job and was always broke. Even after I stopped buying new stuff.

"I'm not much of a consumer," he answered. "I get books at the library, download or swap music, and anything else I need I can trade favors or things I'm not using. Or the universe comes through."

earthgirl

"The universe comes through? You do realize that sounds completely wacko to most normal, sane people?"

"And are you a normal, sane person?" he asked seriously.

"Sometimes. Most of the time, probably."

"Well, it only sounds whacked to people who don't believe it," he shrugged with a small smile. "It brought me you, didn't it?"

I heard a small gasp that sounded like a sex sigh. When it was obvious I was the source of the sound, I realized I was on the verge of choking or asphyxiating or at the very least falling off the wobbly-legged stool then and there.

When I opened my lips to breathe again, instead of the cool, coffee-scented air of the café, I felt Vray's warm, coffee-tasting mouth against mine. Again! The warm moisture of the air in his mouth as his lips pressed perfectly and passionately against mine. AND STAYED THERE!!!

I wobbled slightly on the teetering stool and nearly fell over as his hand reached out and tugged gently at my hair. My eyes darted open and for a minute it was completely Meta. This crazed out-of-body experience where I was hovering over us as he cupped my flushed face in his warm, strong hands and kissed me.

KISSED kissed me.

I shut my eyes tightly as I felt his tongue slide across my teeth (and was so relieved I'd been to Dad the dentist recently and flossed regularly). Behind my lids everything was swirling in rich shades of green and blue, like the trees were melting into the sky and the sea.

Finally I understood.

This was what all the fuss was about.

e a r t h g i r l
do you care-a-boo?
[Oct. 28th | 11:22pm]
[mood | awed]
[music | brother down – sam *swoon* roberts]

Animals are smart, but they get confused when something
is different. Like suddenly there's a BIG HONKING OIL
PIPELINE blocking their path. The route they've taken for
their whole entire creature lives!

So they hang out trying to figure it out. To figure out if
there's another way to go to where they're going. For lunch.
Or a swim. Or maybe some mating action. And it can take
a long time. And they starve or get attacked by wolves.

AND SUDDENLY THERE AREN'T ANYMORE CARIBOU.

Guess most people don't really worry about that much
when they drive their gas guzzlin jalopies or big honking
SUVs to the corner store for chips or to rent a DVD or to
pick up Rover from his doggy daycare and spa!

FYI caribou are cousins of reindeer. So when they're gone,
who pulls Santa's sleigh? A pickup truck? A pack of
elves? No one?

link   read 4 | post
www.cariboucommons.com

earthgirl

altalake 10-28 23:58
The link to the caribou site with the letter
from Robert Redford and the spooky music was
haunting. Cariboo-hoo. :(

"We've already given a deposit," Mom said, as if that would change my mind.

"I'll pay you back from my job," I answered. It wasn't exactly what I had in mind for my hard-earned cashola, but seemed only fair under the circumstances.

"That's not the point, Sabine," Dad said in his very logical voice, which he annoyingly seemed to be using a lot more than usual lately. "You need to take driving lessons to get your licence and ensure the best rates on insurance. Otherwise it's ridiculous for a first-time teen driver."

"You don't get it, Daddy," I sighed. "You don't have to worry about expensive insurance. I don't want my driver's licence."

"You can't wait to drive," Mom snorted. "You've been counting the days since your tenth birthday."

"I changed my mind," I replied. "I have a whole different perspective on cars and driving now."

"Don't be silly. You'll change your mind back. And what about Ella? She'll be so disappointed."

"It's not like she won't be able to learn to drive without me taking the course, too," I scoffed.

"Actually, kiddo, I'm not sure I agree with you," Daddy smirked. "She's not exactly the sharpest knife in the drawer."

"Bob!" Mom scolded. "Don't say things like that about Beana's friends."

"Please," I groaned.

"I just don't understand where this is coming from all of a sudden. It's like that stupid woman and her garbage gave you brain damage," Mom said. "First it was the new job, then you stop flushing the toilet and now this from a girl who used to beg me to drive her to the mall so she didn't have to take the bus? Something's up."

Then, like a complete freak, she knelt down in front of me and took my face in her hands and stared me straight in the eyeballs.

"You're not doing drugs or something crazy," she demanded, her nose to my nose.

"For Pete's sake, Rachel, leave the girl alone," Dad said. "If she's so smart she thinks she doesn't need to drive that's her decision. Personally I think she's being ridiculous, but that's what teenagers do, right?"

"Thank you," I answered, pulling my face away from my mother's clammy grasp. "And for your information, it's exactly like me. The new, improved I'm-part-of-this-planet-and-I-care-about-it me."

With that I stomped out of the living room, even though stomping on wall-to-wall carpeting wasn't all that dramatic or noisy.

And it would have been the ideal gesture if I hadn't heard my mom swipe my glory moment by muttering to my dad in her know-it-all-mom voice, "This is all your fault. I warned you not to encourage her with that stupid book."

earthgirl
[Nov. 05th | 10:01pm]
[mood | brain ache — is that a mood or mood disorder?]
[music | nothing ever happens — blake babies]

I discovered another new word today — "ECOTAGE" A
hybrid of ECOLOGY and SABOTAGE. It's poo-poo-ed by
some people in green circles as destructive and harsh.
Others deem it necessary. Imperative.

There is also "environmental advocacy." And "environmental
activism." I'm not sure what the difference is. It probably
depends on who uses the word. Or who points the finger.
Or which side you think you are on.

The weird thing is that people are actually on different
sides in this one. Aren't we all on the same side?

The side of kindess, decency and survival?

link   read 6 | post
www.saveourclimate.ca

lacklusterlulu 11.05 10:57
Me myself and I advocate activism and positivism but not
nepotism. Cept for me.

MachFhive II-05 II:33
I'm on the side of using freeks like U for animal testing. Why waste a
good rat?

earthgirl   82

altalake 11-05 21:38
buddy, take it somewhere else. sorry you feel
green washed by the truth, but get over it.

e a r t h g i r l
[Nov. 06th | 4:36pm]
dont fret it alta. at least we know which side HE's on!

eight_

"My parents are buying me a Mini," Carmen announced, waving a very glossy brochure at me and Ella as we stood by our lockers moments before first period and mere seconds after her morning smooch-and-grope with Darren (strategically staged practically *licking* distance from our faces... *uck!*).

This was the perfect time to break my news about ditching driving school to Ella, but I held my tongue. I'd tell her later, so I didn't throw off her entire day. Plus I didn't want to hijack Carmen's bragging, especially since it gave me a great opportunity to slip in some tasty socially conscious tidbits.

"Why don't you get a Smart Car?" I asked, since if Carmen had hypnotized or tantrumed her parentals into buying her a car, she could easily sway them to get a caring car.

"What's so smart about a car that only holds two people and a sandwich bag?"

"It's electric," I said, pretty certain it was, or at least very eco-kind.

"I'll wait till they come out with a solar car," she shrugged, tucking the colorful pamphlet in her purple binder.

"They have," Ella grinned. "It's called a bike!"

I couldn't help but smile. The comment was pretty sharp for Ella, who had a tendency to be pretty dim (okay, bad metaphor in light of the quite good solar joke). Sadly, despite their charms and senses of humor, it was growing ever more obvious (and slightly frustrating) that converting my gals to my new way of thinking was going to be a long, slow process.

I shouldn't really have been surprised.

With all the hype and urgency the environment, weather, food supply and water were generating everywhere these days, it was inevitable my girlz would switch to tune out. Or skeptical at least. Green fatigued. And who could blame them? Even I was occasionally exhausted by the breathless, overmedicated news-spewing talking heads and undermedicated political hacks spitting out URGENT warnings. Not to mention the flippant nature of ultra-spoiled celebs driving away from gift-bag-a-ramas in their sparkling Prius's (Priui?) hybrids. And I'd sniffed out the paradox of people with multiple homes scarfing down endangered sea bass at swishy charity fundraisers.

Yup, if Carmen and Ella were indicative of anything, it was the fickle yet shrewd and discriminating nature of my peeps. Of my entire generation. And the importance of working from the inside out.

Thankfully, I was an insider. A long-time and most importantly beloved (if occasionally lovingly mocked) insider.

"Maybe if we rattled some cages we'd care less about cars and driving," I said, with what I hoped sounded like equal parts humor and wisdom.

Ella elbowed Carmen and huffed a little laugh.

"What?"

"Nothing," Ella said, making it abundantly clear it was definitely something. "Carmee and me have a little wager that you'd do this, that's all."

"You keep hanging on to all this blah, blah, blah inconvenient truth stuff. We sat through those lectures, too. We're fine with the Kyoto or fritchin' Toyota protocols, but it's not up to us, Sabine," Carmen explained calmly. "We're at the bottom of the food chain and if corporations and governments sit on their asses, me using a plastic fork won't end the world."

"Fine. Make fun of me, but slagging off personal responsibility lets them get away with their corruption. They're accountable to us, you know. We live in a democracy."

"We can't even vote and we can barely drive," Ella said bluntly.

"And most of us don't have jobs or pay taxes," Carmen continued. "Trust me, it's sweet of you to get all riled up, but no one in power gives a flyer."

"They will," I said confidently. "Oh, I almost forgot. I got you guys a prezzie." I reached into my backpack and grabbed the thoughtful new gifts. One for Carmen, one for Ella and one for me to signify friendship, solidarity and taking care of the planet.

"What's this?" Carmen asked, tangling and untangling her French manicured talons from the unbleached organic cotton mesh.

"A stringbag," I beamed. "From the co-op. They're fair trade."

"What for?"

"To keep in your purse or your pack, in case you buy something."

"If I buy something, they give me a bag," Carmen said, handing it back.

I put my hand out to block her.

"This way they don't have to," I explained as Ella played with hers, stretching it, then springing it back to its contracted size like a kid.

"Yeah," Carmen nodded. "Except they want to and I want them to."

"And you create more garbage."

"No, I don't. I use that Guess bag from when I got that silky top. I brought it to your house when I gave you my old CosmoGirls and Vogues. Okay, maybe not the Banana Republic bag, but it's just a normal shopping-bag bag. Though the one from the Betsey Johnson store is cute."

"That's a really nice one," Ella agreed.

"You guys don't get it, do you?" I sighed.

"We get it," Ella insisted. "You want to be Sabine the green, so we're supposed to be excited. But we're not. Sorry."

"Why?" I asked, genuinely confused.

"Look, we've been through this already and it sucks you got beaned with trash, but it's not our fault the world is going to hell in a handbasket or a breadbasket or whatever," Carmen shrugged. "And just to be clear, I'd rather have fun and live and buy stuff than spend my time worrying and marching around whining."

"I'm not whining," I said, hoping I wasn't. "I just think this is important. It's life or death."

"No, you think it'll impress the wild boy with the stupid name," Carmen said. "And when you get over him, you'll gravitate to the next thing. It's no biggie. We all do it. You don't actually think I like watching Darren's basketball practice? Or sitting there while he plays that iBox crap?"

"XBox."

"Exactly," she shrugged. "Girl's gotta do what a girl's gotta do."

"How is the solar hottie, anyway?" Ella asked.

"Not that I feel like discussing it because you clearly don't get me or any of this, but he's amazing," I answered, trying to tell them a lot without telling them anything. "And for the record, I was interested in the state of the world before I even met Vray."

"Then it's good you found each other so you can have long gushy chats about windmills and soybeans," Carmen agreed. "Cause as much as we love you, we're really hoping the old Sabine comes back from the bush soon cause the lectures are getting a little lame."

And with that she flung the stringbag back at me like a slingshot.

e a r t h g i r l
blow it out your...
[Nov 11th | 8:34pm]
[mood | confused]
[music | The Closer I Get – Hayden]

Why don't we have more windmills? Why don't we all have
solar panels on our roofs to heat our houses and our
water? Hello? The sun and the wind are FREE!!!!

And they aren't going away – at least NOT IN OUR LIFE-
TIMES.

Instead we use OIL. We fight wars for it. We pollute the
world with it. And we act like the earth is a tap that will
always run full tilt to feed our greedy SUV tanks. And the
tank tanks that storm through the desert to protect "FREE-
DOM."

Freedom is a synonym for OIL. And here's the irony. There
isn't an endless supply. The world is running out!! 80% of
the oil in the world was found before 1973! Years and
years before most of us were even born!! Way way way
before apples, cellphones and guitar hero. Or even laptops,
CDs and VCRs if you can believe it?!

It's funny, we found all these ways to update technology to
make our lives better and faster and compactor and new
and improved. But somehow we've turned away from the
SUN and the WIND which are out there RIGHT IN OUR
FACES EVERY SINGLE DAY. Whispering and occasionally

SHOUTING the secrets of their powers and we're too stupid to listen.

link   read 7 | post

onederful 11-11 10:04
Today on remembrance day, important things
to remember in addition to the brave people
who fought for our freedom. We harvest less
than 3% of the world's energy from the sun.
But all is not lost in some enlightened
places. Iceland harnesses thermodynamic
power from steaming vents underground.
Denmark gets 20% of its power from windmills and hopes to make that 50% soon. And
Portugal is building the world's largest
solar power station. Obrigado! (that's
thank you in Portuguese)
www.solarbuzz.com

altalake 11-11 21:33
Obviously the sun always shines in Portugal!
Remember your UV sunscreen hat and water (in a
refillable BPA-free bottle!)

"What's going on?" Dad asked as he slammed his car
door shut with the kind of purpose that suggested he wanted attention. Immediately.

"Finn and Vray are helping move the fridge to the curb."

I explained what was clearly obvious, but obviously in need of explaining.

"That much I can see," Dad answered, taking in the scene on our front lawn. "I probably should have asked why you and your shaggy new buddies are dumping my beer fridge."

"It's an energy-guzzling piece of junk, Daddy," I answered, gesturing toward what used to be the fridge, but was now a hulking box of open metal, a door and some rust-tinged shelving and drawers.

"Sabine's right," Vray chimed in. "It's ancient and might even have CFCs. Very toxic and surprisingly expensive to run."

"Thank you..." Dad paused leaning forward a bit and waiting for a response from Vray.

"Vray, Vray Foret. Good to meet you, sir," he answered, wiping his rusty, gooky hands on his thighs and shaking my dad's.

"It was my idea, actually," I announced. "Vray and Finn were just helping me. And I called the city to pick it up so don't worry. They'll be here Wednesday."

"Sabine, I don't want to embarrass you in front of your new friends," Dad said, pulling me aside a bit and speaking in his best Dad voice. "But I didn't ask you to do this and, at the very least, you should have asked me."

"But you'd have said no," I answered.

"You're right. That's why you should have asked."

"Um, Mr. Solomon, if you don't mind me saying so." Finn waded calmly into the middle. "Ditching this clunker will save heaps of money in the long run, both in terms of electricity costs and spoiled beer. I mean, quality beer – and

91   **earthgirl**

I'll go out on a limb here and figure you for the quality stuff – doesn't really last longer than a month or two, so no sense storing too much."

"You've forgotten the additional costs of driving to the beer store more often since I now don't have a beer fridge, antique or otherwise," Dad answered. "And aren't you a bit young to be drinking?"

"I don't," Finn answered. "My sister's boyfriend told me about the stale thing."

"You don't even like beer much," Mom's voice chimed from the door to the garage. "Besides, it'll free up space for the rest of your junk."

"See?" I said. "Everyone is happy."

"Not quite, honey. You still haven't introduced me to your new boyfriend," Mom replied.

I cringed when she said the word. Not that I didn't like to think that maybe Vray was my boyfriend. It's just that he never precisely said he was, and now suddenly she was announcing it right in front of him and his BMF. It was epically embarrassing and made me wish I were an ostrich with the power to drill my head into driveway pavement.

"Let me guess, you must be Vray," she beamed, walking down the three steps toward us and straight for Finn who, though not exactly clean cut, was the tidier of the pair.

"Actually Mrs. S., that'd be me," Vray said as he tried to tuck in his overstretched T-shirt and gave me a wink. "Sabine's told me a lot about you."

"I'm sure she has," Mom said, leaning in coyly and practically *flirting*! "Mysteriously, she hasn't told us much about you, so I think you'll have to stay for dinner. And your moving buddy, too."

"It's Finn, and thanks, but I've gotta go," Finn answered. "I'm volunteering at the animal shelter tonight."

"That's really good of you," Mom said, sounding genuinely impressed.

"Not really," Finn replied. "I'm just trying to find homes for abandoned animals so they don't get snuffed. Ticking clock down there."

And then Finn gave Vray one of those strange, secret, guy club props handshakes and patted him on the back. His bike was by the curb, where the remains of the fridge now lay in pieces. He jumped on it and rode off waving behind him.

By this point Mom had gathered up Dad and his gym bag of squash gear and was herding him up the front path.

"Haven't you told him about me?" Vray asked after the parentals had gone back into the house to no doubt dish and scheme.

"Not exactly," I answered, though not at all would have been more accurate.

"Why not?"

"Cause he's my dad and he's so embarrassing, as you just witnessed."

"He's just a dad," Vray shrugged. "And it might have been nice if you'd told him about me so I wouldn't forever be known as 'the boy who trashed my beer fridge.'"

"You're right. I'm sorry. I'm just new at all this. The boyfriend-girlfriend thing, the getting-rid-of-unnecessary-stuff thing. That trying-to-change-the-world-and-be-a-better-person thing. All of it."

"It's okay," Vray said, sweeping me up into one of his delicious knee-buckling hugs. "You can tell people I exist. I'm not going anywhere."

"So then," I paused, feeling elated and exhausted all at once, "you are my boyfriend?"

He laughed and squeezed me. And suddenly, all I could think of besides melting into his arms was running away with him and living in a big treehouse above the forests and fields with the blue sky and the birds and animals all around us. Totally cornball and ridiculous, but I guess that's what love does. It makes you crazy and silly. And, sometimes if you're supremely lucky, it makes you care in a whole new way.

• • •

As if I needed to be more amazed and impressed, Vray handled dinner like a complete pro. I figured he'd been blindsided by the invitation and nervous to boot. But he wasn't the teeniest bit thrown or ruffled by my embarrassing parentals or my cringingly nosy sister. Maybe it was all the practice he'd had with his own mom and dad's friends, but he was totally surprising. In only the best possible ways.

When my mom offered him a roast beef sandwich slathered in globby synthetic gravy, instead of going off about cruel practices in the cattle industry, he simply and very politely settled for some tomato slices on a bun. And not even a whole grain bun.

Definite bonus points for excellent table manners to cancel points lost for chucked fridge fiasco.

"They're not organic or even local," I whispered to the side of his face, trying not to breathe in the grassy lime smell of his hair, in case I fainted in front of my entire family. "I'm trying to convince her, but she usually just goes to the superstore up on Yonge Street and even then straight to the cheap stuff."

"It's more convenient," Mom shot back, giving me the hairy eyeball. (I never realized she could lip read or had such spooky good ears.) "I told you to bring food home from the co-op if it's so important to you. Baby steps, kiddo, baby steps."

"It's okay," he said, giving my thigh a little pat under the table. "I'm pretty adaptable."

"What's the deal with your name?" Clare asked.

"It's just a name," Vray said, offering her his killer smile.

"A stupid name." Clare snorted what I'm pretty sure my parents were probably thinking, too, but were too civilized to point out.

"Clare, Vray's a guest," Dad said in a tone that actually sounded like he was trying to not laugh.

"I know," she said, her head bobbing and her mouth full of roast beef and bun mush. "A guest with a dumb name, no offense."

"None taken," Vray answered. The guy's technique with parents and stupid sisters was a marvel to behold.

Later when we were finally sprung from dinner and went upstairs, I realized it was the first ever time I'd had a boy I

95   **earthgirl**

actually liked in my room. As it was, boy visits were few and far between except for the occasional homework assignment or my neighbor Kenny hanging out playing crazy eights or backgammon when we were twelve. And even though my parents could be freakishly random at times, I was happy I didn't have some goofy rule about male visitors. Carmen's mom wouldn't even let Darren go upstairs, as if that would stop them from making out like minxes any chance they got.

Vray was lounging back on my bed getting comfy, which included crushing my darling Pokemon plushy behind his back. I watched, unsure whether to alert him, but decided it would sound babyish. It was, after all, a pillow. A pillow that along with Chichi and his fake furry friends should have been exiled to a time way before boys lounged in my room, on my bed with me. Oopsy.

"Someone should invent a videogame like Grand Theft Auto but instead of car thieves, the dudes are eco-warriors blowing away polluters and corporate assholes ruining the planet. Then all the carnage would have a point, carnage for carnage," he said as he squished the yellow blob into a comfy position behind his dreamy mop of curls.

"Like an eye for an eye?" I asked, trying to figure out if he was joking or serious.

"Yeah, that might be the best way to get people to change. I mean, you yelling at that lady in Kensington was amusing, but in the end it didn't achieve much, even with the web exposure."

"So you want to threaten and hurt people?" I wondered, sitting down at the foot of the bed and looking at him lounging there all cozy on my bed. In my room. ON MY BED!

"Maybe. The really bad ones. Now come here and kiss me or I'll have to tickle you for a week." He tugged on my belt loop to bring me closer to him.

"My parents are downstairs!" I said, trying to be shocked, but unable to wipe the massive smile off my face. I was terrified and excited, the little electrical shocks sparking in my fingertips again.

As soon as I slumped down on top of him, his mouth was against mine again. Soft and warm and wet and delicious and dizzying, and I started to forget where I was or how I got there or what he'd even said a few minutes before. His gorgeous, daring hands twisting under my T-shirt, pressing and flicking against my tummy. My barenaked tummy!

"Ah! Gross!" Clare groaned at the door. "Get a room."

"Do you mind!" I shouted bolting up from where I was melted against Vray's warm chest. "This is a room, *my* room and there's something called knocking?!"

"Dad wants to know if Vray wants a ride home," she said as I adjusted my tangled shirt back to almost normal.

"A ride would be great," Vray said, not the least bit embarrassed that we'd been caught necking madly.

"Um, in the car? With my dad?" I was a little freaked he'd willingly subject himself to that.

"Fine, I'll go tell him," Clare said, even though she stood in the doorway gawking like she was glued to the spot.

"Why not? I'll put my bike in the trunk and this way you've got me at your mercy for a few more minutes."

"Ah, Clare, you can leave anytime now," I said, glaring at my sister.

"Gladly," she snapped backing out the door without closing it.

I definitely needed to get a lock.

e a r t h g i r l
[Nov. 14th | 10:25pm]
[mood | duped]
[music | Don't Believe the Hype — Public Enemy]
The monkey wrench gang are not real. Not the terrono punk band who do actually exist, i've seen 'em in concert and have the bleeding ears to prove it. Turns out the "not real" Monkeywrench gang of the eco-warrior variety are actually made up characters from a novel about people who blow up bridges and reek other eco-havoc.

They do have a real life, vigilante equivalent. the Earth Liberation Front! (ELF) and Animal Liberation Front! (ALF) exist and advocate "monkeywrenching" AKA fooking wid da seestem.

Is it just me, or is it strange that 2 X-treme eco-orgs have cutsy-wootsy names like ELF and ALF. I wonder if that's supposed to be ironic. Probably, IRONY seems to be very big these dayz. At least in my universe.

link   read 7 | post

altalake 11-15 00:04
Irony is the new sincerity.

onederful 11-15 01:31
Irony is good. Ironing, not so good. So
embrace your wrinkles they've embraced you.

Vague-a-bond 11-16 21:21
"Sentiment without action is the ruin of the soul." – Edward
Abbey, author + activist, The Monkeywrench Gang. I
looooovvvveeee that book. Thought it was sooo funny. Luv the
blog greenbean. Inspired. Always.
lacklusterlulu 11-15 14:13
Actually alta, irony is the new black!

nine_

Biggish news on the normally not hugely newsworthy academic frontier. Cue the drum roll and guitar solo...

I got my very first ever A plus! Yes, that's right, an A and a plus! And the crowd goes wild! The crowd of me, anyway.

This historic event occurred in social studies for my cleverly titled paper, "Global Warning." It also proves two significant things: (1) it definitely helps to actually care about, or at least be remotely interested in the subjects you are studying and (2) never underestimate the power of a well-placed pun.

"Printing on the back of used paper was a nice touch, Sabine," Mr. Sarrazin noted as he handed back my assignment.

"Thanks," I beamed as I saw the eye-popping never-before-seen mark at the top of the page beside my name. "It made sense considering our history of pollution since the Industrial Revolution."

"Timely and urgent without histrionics, well done," he nodded. "I also like your ideas for small contributions we can all make toward solving this crisis."

I sat proudly at my desk electrified by the compliments.

Who knew there were side benefits to my eco-interests, like actually doing better-than-okay in school?!

My smoocherific boyfriend would be so pleased. He was so helpful pointing me toward excellent reference sources. He was so clever. It was very sexy. And inspiring. And intense. Oh, and did I mention sexy?

"So what's the deal on Be Green Day," the normally elusive and reclusive Shane McCardle asked as we left Sarrazin's class, marking the second time he'd talked to me since The Incident.

Be Green Day was the me-initiated effort to promote and increase recycling on school grounds, build awareness of excessive excess, culminating in a garbage gathering jaunt along the beltway trail through the middle of the city. It was mere days away and I was amped to the max.

"Just my way of giving back by taking back," I said, feeling a tad suspicious that Shane's sudden interest was a cruel joke. Or that he was just making some ironic stoner comment.

"Cool, but next time you might think about doing it in the spring instead," he said, faking a shiver.

"Didn't you know? With global warming November is the new April," I joked, only then realizing that spring actually would have been better.

"Funny girl," he said, nodding and gliding away down the hall like an apparition of some exotic tribe.

As he disappeared, the defensiveness and tension I'd been holding in my neck and shoulders escaped like a sigh. It appeared that some people actually did give a hoot about my ideas. People like Shane. Which shouldn't have surprised me since he was at Vray's concert and it definitely couldn't have been for the music.

Finally, despite the sniggers and groans after the morning PA announcement, a small rally of support. And with Shane McCardle's high-level recognition and awe factor, things were certainly looking up.

• • •

At lunch Carmen and Ella descended on me like vultures with uncharacteristically blank expressions. They each looped an arm through mine and led me out of the school.

"What's up? We going for Thai?" I asked.

"Not exactly," Carmen said.

"Cause Thai food would be a great way to celebrate my brilliant A plus!" I bragged. "Sushi works, too. Just not tuna, too much mercury."

"We're not celebrating your grades," Ella said sternly. "But congrats anyway."

"Don't encourage her," Carmen huffed.

I braked and yanked my arms from theirs as we hit the sidewalk at the edge of the schoolyard.

"What's going on?" I asked. "You're freaking me out here."

"We're freaking you out?" Carmen said. "Little Miss Birkenstock-sock-face says we're freaking her out?"

"It's an intervention," Ella nodded.

"This is a joke, right?"

"It's not, Bean," Ella answered solemnly.

"We begged you to stop all the sky-is-falling crap, but you're like Chicken Little running around screaming after he got pinged with a pine cone," Carmen said in a tone that managed to sound oddly preachy, well-informed, judgmental, mean and loving at the same time.

"But the sky *is* falling," I answered calmly. "In a way."

"Were you pinged by a pine cone?" Ella parted my hair and examined my scalp for a second before I shook her free. "You could use a color touch, sweetie. Gnarly rootage."

"I don't care. Hair color is full of toxic chemicals," I said, flicking her hands away. "And my vanity isn't worth killing the planet for."

"She's doing it again," Ella said, shaking her head. "It's worse than you thought."

"Seriously Sabine, I hate to be the one to tell you, but you're getting…" Carmen paused for a moment, then sighed dramatically. "Tedious. You're seriously tedious so stop it already. Stop it last week."

"You are." Ella nodded like a bobblehead. "Seriously tedious."

"We tried to be patient and let you blather it out of your system, but it keeps getting worse," Carmen continued, as if the knife needed to be dug in deeper and cranked.

"You used to be fun," Ella added. "Now you act like a teacher or a mom or something…not fun."

"Look, we realize this seems harsh," Carmen said, acting suddenly kind. "But between raising money for homeless people, writing to the UN about Darfur, trying to get good marks and have boyfriends, we're exhausted. We can't take on every fritchin' cause, plus we don't want to. We're your best friends and if we didn't say it, who would?"

"Yeah and it's still early enough to make some new friends if you want," Ella offered helpfully.

"Not that we're trying to ditch you, cause we're not," Carmen intercepted. "What El's trying to say is we love you a ton, well, we love the old you, so can you ask the alien abductors to please bring her back?"

Which if you think about it was a really odd thing to say since I was standing right there in front of them. Talking to them and with them. Or maybe from the way they saw it, talking *at* them.

I felt completely winded. I didn't know what to say. So for the first time in eons, I said nothing. I just nodded and smiled a sad little smile. My two very best and oldest friends were attacking what was the new core of my very being. And they thought they were doing me a favor!

"So?" Carmen stood there with her hands on her hips. "Aren't you going to say anything?"

"No," I shrugged. "It's pretty clear you aren't interested in what I have to say."

"That's not what we're saying," Ella backpedaled.

Carmen let out a long, exasperated sigh.

"Yeah, but it doesn't have to be like this."

"It's okay," I said, trying to keep my voice from wavering and clasping my clammy hands together behind my back so they wouldn't see them shake. "I get it. It's all overwhelming. You need to make choices. I hear you and it's cool."

If Carmen and Ella actually thought this childish, crappy intervention idea was going to change my mind about things that were life and death important to me now, they were wrong. If they expected me to sacrifice the entire planet for our friendship, I guess they didn't value the planet as much as I did. Or value me and my new values. And I guess their friendship didn't mean as much to me as it once did.

I turned and started walking down the hallway. I was so tempted to look back, but knew that would be a huge mistake. And I'd probably lose what tiny fragment of composure and dignity I was managing to hang on to.

It was confounding and strange. Not to mention profoundly sad. The end of an era. But the farther away I moved, the lighter I actually felt.

e a r t h g i r l
the reason of voice
[Nov. 16th | 4:44pm]
[mood | misunderstood]
[music | Bulletproof I wish I was... — Radiohead]

Now I understand how poor Joan of Arc must have felt. Well, except for the hearing voices part.

Though if you stop to consider this venue, everyone who posts here is a kind of voice. A voice that I Sabine of North Toronto hear, but a lot of other people are incapable of hearing. Or just ignore. :(

Maybe this is just the modern equivalent of hearing voices. And maybe I'm just bracing for battles that will be won. Hope so.

It would suck to sacrifice so much and gain so little.

link   read 4 | post
www.earthcare.org

lacklusterlulu 11-16 10:57
**Um earthgirlfriend, the way I learned it, little soldier Joanie
heard the voice of, well...you know – the BIG GAL. I'm flattered
you consider us in that realm but we're really just like you –
small voices in the big wilderness while there still is a wilderness.**

earthbound01 11-17 10:36
Not to mention large suckage being burned at the stake. So what if
they admit they goofed, yer still toast.

"Check this," Clare said, dancing around the kitchen
with a shiny new turquoise toxic-spewing supermop con-
traption.

"A regular mop does the same thing," I snapped. Despite
my repeated pleas, improved grades and general fabulous-
ness, my stupid family still behaved like environmental hea-
thens.

"Doesn't do this," Clare answered flipping it up and
shoving it in my face to show off the dust bunnies, hair
clumps and icky food detritus stuck to the disposable diaper-
like pad. "Just like the commercials say!"

"Finally, truth in advertising," Mom said, stepping in
and unclipping the grotty pad to replace it with a fresh,
crispy clean one.

"I can't believe this," I half sighed, half ranted.

"Me either. Clare's never cleaned anything in her life," Mom said, kissing her on the forehead. "It's truly a miracle of modern innovation."

"No," I said forcefully. "That you buy into all this supposed timesaving earth-wrecking crap. What's the use of saving time if we don't have any left?"

"Look, sweetie, I'm sorry your green enviro thing at school isn't setting the world on fire, but in case you forgot, I'm the boss around here and I happen to like, no *love* the supermop. A lot!"

"Is it really asking so much to use environmentally friendly cleaners?"

"Not if you clean the house," she snapped. "In case you hadn't noticed, I have a full-time job, two demanding teenage girls and a husband who expect me to do everything around here."

"That's not fair. I help out, I empty the dishwasher, I clean my room, I shovel snow, I'm a good daughter," I said, defending my efforts which somehow didn't sound as lofty when I listed them off like that.

"Okay, Sabine, I'm trying to be supportive, but I've had enough," Mom sighed. "If it's not the food I buy, it's the fridge or antibacterial soap that's bad. Would you please give it a rest already."

"Antibacterial soap is bull. It causes more problems and diseases because we need bacteria and it's stupid to pretend otherwise. It's been on the news. Ask your husband the dentist. He makes a living from bacteria."

"And I'm going to pretend that the old sweet cooperative Sabine Olivia Solomon still lives here rather than this new royal pain in the ass," Mom snapped, marching off with the mop like an army general. "I sure hope you don't go off on your friends like this."

Ouch.

Clare shrugged, rolled her eyes and stuck her pocky pink tongue out at me. I went to grab it the way we used to when we were kids, but she sucked it back into her mouth before I could. Then she marched after Mom like a stupid lemming. Hurling themselves off the cliff onto the rocky garbage-strewn shores below. Splat, splat, crunch, splat.

And here I was standing at the top of the mountain looking out over the land and the sea trying to enjoy the view.

Alone.

e a r t h g i r l
[Nov. 18th | 10:01pm]
[mood | dazzled]
[music | Snowblink – Oh My Avalanche]

I must direct you to a super cool site. THE RUCKUS SOCIETY!!! It's an incredible resource for active, engaging, nonviolent protest action – like scaling buildings to hang giant banners (that aren't selling products!!!) Imagine!

They have something called ACTION CAMP. I mean seriously forget *band camp* or regular sleepaway camp. They teach you to climb things and organize rallies.

Sadly, it's highly doubtful the units will sign the necessary documentation for me to attend in the near near future. But I'm softening 'em up. okay trying. And failing that, when the clock strikes – 18! – I'm so there!!! Watch for the earthgirl repelling/rappelling (sp?) from a building near you soon.

link   read 4 | post
www.ruckus.org

lorax 11-18 23:58
Too bad the Truffula trees didn't have future ruckus campers like you. I'd never have had to leave my lovely forest. Darn the needs for Thneeds indeed.
wikipedia.org/wiki/The_Lorax

Besides the co-op, my relationship with Vray was about the only redeeming thing I had going on. And since my new quest was to be the best me possible, how could that not include being an awesome GF and all that entailed?

So it was with great glee and surprise that I emerged through the funky gloom and saw a mountain to conquer. Well, metaphorically, anyway, since it was actually a fake one at the indoor rock climbing gym.

Hard to believe my striving-to-be-hip mother had first suggested such a rad plan last March break. At the time I hadn't paid much attention, mainly because Carmen and Ella scoffed when I threw it out there, convincing me to join them for a pointless shopping romp and an all-the-rage gross-out sweaty yoga class instead.

Suddenly, an introductory climbing course seemed like a great way to spend another co-op-less Saturday afternoon now that I had an abundance of friend-free time and a boyfriend to adore and impress.

"The weekend doesn't work," Vray said later on the phone when I suggested we take it together.

We spent a lot of time on the phone when we weren't together, which was sadly too often since he went to Jarvis Collegiate, a cool downtown high school. Plus he only talked on landlines because he found the cell's "voodoo monitoring, constant upgrades and enforced obsolescence an obscene aspect of our consumer-mad disposable culture." And he only occasionally wrote emails plus wasn't into IM-ing. He preferred using online time for serious research.

I preferred lying in bed with the phone to my ear listening to the purring of his voice to the cold sameness of reading words on a computer screen. Even if my mother called me retro and Clare the mouth-breather accidentally-on-purpose picked up at least once per call.

"What's going on?" I asked.

"Just some stuff. Me and Finn and Eric have plans."

"I don't think I've met Eric," I said, wondering what these plans might be and why he wouldn't say.

"He plays bass with O-Zone," he answered.

"Oh." I was afraid that if I asked another question, Vray might think I was being a nosy jealous girlfriend (and not the only slightly nosy and not-at-all-jealous girlfriend I actually was).

"Action hero stuff," he said, like he was reading my mind.

"Can I help?" I felt like I should put my money where my mouth was, as it were. And also partly because I didn't have anything else to do now that Carmen and Ella were absent from my universe.

"No, it's cool. You should do the climbing thing."

"I can climb another time. I'd rather hang with you guys, meet Eric and that." I hoped I didn't sound desperate to be with him all the time.

"It's the guys, Sabine. We've had it on deck for a while. Just give it a rest, okay?"

"Yeah, anyway I gotta go. I have a ton of work to do organizing cleanup crews, routes and schedules for Be Green Day," I said, so it seemed like I was the one ending the conversation.

"Right on," he said. "Hope it's a blast and sorry about this. We'll do something fun next weekend, promise."

"Okay," I said, hanging up the phone and wondering if he meant it. And hating myself for having doubts.

About him, about us, and about me.

e a r t h g i r l
Go much much further...
[Nov. 19th | 11:03pm]
[mood | righteous]
[music | stutter – andy stochansky]

In light of my sorry social life, I opted to enjoy a socially conscience movie marathon to further immerse myself in the "so called" world of *alternative thinking.*

Thinking that really oughta be more mainstream, if you actually THINK about it.

First off, THE CORPORATION, this stunning and oh-so-smart indictment of consumer culture, brand brainwashing and all things globalization that should be must watch viewing for EVERYONE. My "CONSUMED" sister especially.

Movie two – GO FURTHER, with that Woody guy from those endless unfunny reruns of Cheers. It could have indeed gone way, way further instead of focusing on some goofy junk food junkie sidekick who just wanted to be in a movie. Lame.

Easy for Woody Harrleson to ride around in a hemp powered bus, toking up, doing yoga and have a chef make raw vegan meals, he's a rich movie star. And he doesn't live with my MOM! Oh well, I guess if one person is enlightened or awakened from the slumber of the masses, that's something.

Even if it's NOT enough.

link   read 3 | post
www.thecorporation.com
www.voiceyourself.com

altalake 11-23 18:54
The Corpse was SCARY good. I recommend "An Inconvenient Truth" about "Who Killed The

Electric Car" at "The Eleventh Hour" while "Manufacturing Landscapes" after "Darwin's Nightmare."

ten_

The volunteer turnout for BGD was a joke. A bad, sad, unfunny joke. Only after the principal, Mrs. Rubin, made participation mandatory for anyone with spares did things happen. And then only barely and with an enthusiasm best described as muted. And since it was actually a warmish sunny day, I couldn't blame the lack of cooperation on the weather.

Sad and strange. Some schools even have environmental clubs and this kind of thing is completely normal. Guess it's because those kids live in British Columbia, Washington State or Oregon, and when you're surrounded by walls of mountains and trees, you see and think about it more.

Carmen and Ella continuing to ignore me in the halls didn't help. But they topped themselves by sneaking away to Ella's house to watch TMZ and YouTube instead of helping to clean up the community. I know because Carmen made a point of announcing their intentions loudly enough for me to hear when Mrs. Rubin was conveniently out of earshot.

Needless to say, I wasn't the most popular girl in the school.

"This is so lame, Solomon," Corey Crawford complained.

"Shane McCardle isn't whining," I snapped back after observing Shane and his homies dragging back stuffed trash bags. What a rockstar.

"Cause he's high," Darren Mankowsky said with serious snark.

Even if it were true, that was nobody's business. My business, however, was getting my fellow students to separate the in-school garbage for recycling (not exactly taxing) and then share a few minutes during lunch to help clean up litter in the 'hood. Which was ridiculously difficult even when I handed out work gloves that I'd had generously donated by Thompson's Hardware (after three visits and a lot of begging). Then, in a last-minute burst of inspiration, Mr. T. threw in a white paper jumpsuit for me to wear because it looked like an emergency Hazmat suit and he thought it might get me and my efforts on the news.

Good plan in theory, though it didn't exactly work getting media attention. And it only got me more snide comments.

I'm not sure what I expected given that garbage-in-the-face on YouTube didn't wrestle people from their complacent dazes.

I didn't assume it would be a raging success, but I hardly expected it to be such a fiasco. It's like they'll spend twenty bucks to go to some yoga class to bend down like doggies, but no one could be bothered to bend over and pick wrappers off the ground.

Though something oddly happy did happen when scary anorexic Alexis Shaw came up to me afterwards.

"I really admire what you're doing," she said, touching me on the arm with her very bony fingers.

"Careful," I warned, only half joking. "You wouldn't want anyone else to hear you say that."

"No, seriously. It takes a lot of balls to stand up to all these morons," she said. "I think you're an inspiration. If it weren't for you and all this stuff I'd have never tapped into the raw food diet. It changed my life."

"I'm sure you'd have found it without me," I said, trying to keep my expression as judgment-free as possible. Everyone knew Alexis was totally food obsessed – or not, depending on which perspective you took. And she was still so skinny that you couldn't see her if she turned sideways.

Then again, if she was actually eating food and digesting it that was probably a good start.

"Still, what you're trying to do is pretty cool, even if no one else thinks so," she smiled, melting away into the crowd down the hall.

Maybe I had to learn to be more generous and recognize when people were actually on my side. Or to be more like a duck and not really care what people thought of me, which I was definitely getting more skilled at.

Like my mom liked to say, "You wouldn't care what people thought about you if you knew how little they did!" Meaning, not often.

e a r t h g i r l
[Nov. 25th | 10:01am]
[mood | dumbfounded]
[music | Girls – Eleni Mandell]

Why is it that if something's not quite right, most people
say "it could always be worse." Why don't they say, IT
COULD ALWAYS BE BETTER instead?

I mean, obviously it could always be worse. We could have
to walk around with gas masks on our faces to protect our
lungs. Or the whole family could have to bathe with a cold
bucket of water, as I'm sure some families do somewhere.
Or have no food at all, let alone grocery shelves endlessly
stocked with food packed full of toxic preservatives and
chemicals.

Doesn't anybody want the world to be better? Okay anybody in my school and my little universe besides my awesome BF and the few of you fabulous and worthy creatures who read these thoughts?

What does this say about me? That I'm a lousy judge of
character or just unlucky or pathetic? sorry to rant. mopey
mood.

Saving the world is exhausting me. :(

link   read 8 | post
www.evergreen.ca

earthgirl

Vague-a-bond 11-25 22:22
Don't ever give up green bean. Complacency is the death of us. Optimism is the way to go. So what if the dweebs in your school don't get you yet. Optimum word – YET. It's tough being on the vanguard. I should know. :)

lorax 11-26 03:03
Remember how the Bar-ba-loots played in the shade and ate Truffala Fruits? Stay the way, Queen Sabine, and one day the Bar-ba-loots will frisk about all day again.

onederful 11-26 9:11
Its my name, but its also you!

e a r t h g i r l
[Nov. 26th | 06:45am]
Thanx onederful (and everyone else)! Guess that makes us two-derful! Or make that all-derful!

I had to hand it to my sister. When it came to the minutiae of my social and personal life, she was nothing if not astute. If we were taking bets, I'd have pegged Mom to have noticed the glaring absence of C and E in my life. But nope. I guess she was too preoccupied by the launch of this swanky new boutique hotel her PR company was handling. She worked way too hard sometimes – a good and bad thing on the parental interference meter.

So instead, it was nosy Clare who finally broke me down. She barged in on me in the kitchen where I was making the next day's lunch of organic brown rice with marinated tofu and veggies. It was my new routine now that I was avoiding processed cafeteria food and takeout in general.

"Did you have a fight with Carmella?" she asked, using her nickname for the inseparable girl duo.

"Why do you ask?" I responded as calmly as I could despite the sudden appearance of a glob in the back of my throat.

"First, they're never here bugging me any more. Second, you don't even talk about them and third and most obvious, you've been wearing all your own crummy clothes and look like crap," she said flatly as she munched on some carrots I'd just washed and peeled.

"It's no big deal," I said. "We just kind of see things differently these days."

"You mean *you* do. Everything is all green and clean and stuff."

"I guess."

"So who do you hang out with at school? You don't eat lunch by yourself, do you?" As if eating alone in the cafeteria was the number one worst thing that could happen to someone. Though it was pretty large on the list of high-school horrors.

"No, I have other friends," I said. But just barely.

There was Shane McCardle, who now nodded and half waved whenever he saw me, though he hadn't said much since Be Green Day. Not that he'd actually said much of much before.

And lately I'd taken to eating lunch with, or maybe I

should say *for*, Alexis Shaw and her girlie gaggle. After her post BGD confession, she had somehow glommed onto me. I was surprised to discover that she was actually more interesting than her two-dimensional body suggested. She was actually a classically trained flutist and spent her evenings and weekends studying at the Royal Conservatory! Who knew? Certainly not the old cliquey jump-to-conclusion me I used to be.

"You must feel like such a loser," Clare said. "Lucky you have your boyfriend."

I just nodded.

"He didn't tell you not to be friends with them, did he?" Clare asked suddenly, like she was gathering information for a cult or maybe the Girls Intelligence Agency.

"Of course not. I would never be with a guy who told me what I should and shouldn't do."

"Good, because he's pretty hot and I'm sure he's very persuasive."

"I may be new at the whole boyfriend thing," I said, "but I'm not stupid."

"So no Fancy Pants this year, I guess?" she said, reminding me of the annual holiday gift swap that took place between me, Carmen and Ella.

Every year for the last forever, we would exchange mixed CDs and cute underwear. I hadn't thought about it at all till Clare reminded me. Now I realized with exams and Christmas break a mere blink away, Fancy Pants was also approaching at full throttle.

I just shrugged.

"We could do it if you want. I could buy you big all-cotton granny panties. I'm sure your eco-head boyfriend would find them very sexy!"

"Thanks," I smiled, almost tempted to give her a hug for being so sweet for a change. "But it looks like the days of Fancy Pants are over."

"Figures, just when you might actually need them to lure your guy to your lair."

"Where do you come up with this stuff?" I asked, even though I knew it was all those insidious magazines and websites she cruised for dish and rules to live by.

"I make it my business to be in the know," she said proudly.

"Hate to break it to you Clare-bear, but not so much. See, Vray's actually mad for my stellar mind, cutting-edge politics and fabulous sense of humor and that's why we hang out. It's not just all horny guy stuff."

"Like that'll last."

And I realized that she was probably right. Not that I necessarily wanted it to. It's just I didn't want our first time together to be some fumbling oopsy of being reckless and carried away. Some accident of sex that caused bad feelings and worse memories. On the other hand, meticulously organized wasn't the plan either.

You could say, when Vray and I finally did the big *it*, I wanted it to be spontaneous, but in a planned kind of way.

But right now, mostly, I wanted to be absolutely completely positive that he truly cared about me as a person. That who I was and becoming and what I believed and felt truly was as important to Vray as it was to me. And that I, Sabine Olivia Solomon, was as important to him as he was to me.

As in extremely.

eleven_

A funny odd, not funny ha-ha thing happened today. Shane McCardle asked if I wanted to see David Suzuki, the major scientist and envirovisionary, talk about the planet and what we're doing to it.

"The dude walks the no-footprint walk. You gotta admire that," Shane said in that slow, low tone of his.

"I used to watch his science show on TV with my dad," I answered without actually answering his question about going to the lecture.

"Should be an all right talk. I think you'd get into it."

I smiled, nodded and looked down at my feet. I was flattered and flustered. Flattered because finally I had a fledgling new friend with similar interests who even showed initiative. Flustered because I didn't want to be a goof and say, "You do know I have a boyfriend," like I was some smug girl who assumed every guy who talked to her was after her.

Sure it was just a lecture. But Shane was also compelling and delicious and I was now, finally, a boyfriended girl. It was seemingly non-consequential yet potentially loaded moments like these that really tested my commitment to the cause and my love for Vray.

I stood in front of Shane who bobbed his head gently, like he was listening to music in his brain, as he patiently waited for my answer. My mind was racing. I considered asking if Vray could come, too, but quickly realized that was a bad plan. If he did, Shane might be insulted and if he couldn't, Vray might be jealous. I also mulled over just saying no, but I didn't want Shane to think I wasn't interested in him as a friend. Especially since friends, or anything remotely resembling them, were hardly at a surplus at this particular juncture.

"Do you believe in cosmic coincidences," I asked, hoping to get additional insight into whether the invite was innocent or loaded.

"That a special blend or something?" he smirked.

"No, I mean people or situations popping into your world at these serendipitous, simpatico kind of moments?"

"It's just an invitation to see the guy talk," he answered, looking a tad baffled. "We don't need to hook up, unless you want to."

"I know, that's not what I meant," I blabbered, certain my face was as red as my sweater. "Anyway, it's on Thursday right? I'm pretty sure I have to work at the co-op that night."

It was the first time ever in my life that I lied to someone right to their face. And the way the words popped out of my mouth so easily also suggested it might not be the last.

"Cool. I like that place. They give out free tasters," he answered. "So, I'll let you know how it goes then."

"I'd like that," I said, which was completely true even if the part about working wasn't.

"Later," he nodded, as he sauntered off down the hall in all his laid-back, dreamy glory.

I stood there shaking my head, vowing to myself that if I had to stretch the truth again, even in a small way, it must definitely be for the good of humanity.

e a r t h g i r l
[Dec. 02nd | 8:45pm]
[mood | disillusioned]
[music | As Serious As Your Life | Four Tet]

Politicians are really total fools. I know, I know, I'm stating a totally "doh" obvious thing and all that but here's yet more proof. The local goofs in the otherwise fantastic metropolis known as Toronto (hometown of Stars, Sum 41, Scott Speedman, Ryan Gosling and Ms. Naomi Klein) have decided that POSTERING is an ugly blight/blite/smite? on the city.

Postering, that grass roots, mucho effort practice of walking or riding your bike around with a staple gun and some glue and letting people know about kewl ideas and events.

Bad, bad, bad!

But, get this, GIANORMOUS TV sets and light boards four stories high that blink and glow 24/7 at a major downtown intersection like Yonge + Dundas forcing you to watch commercials for things you don't need and promos for CSI: Universe are... GOOD!

Um? Excuse me?

No wonder people my age don't bother with politics beyond signing online petitions or seeing some honking big concert. Or worse that we don't get our hands dirty or think about being future leaders of the world. Who wants to hang out with such idjits – or worse risk becoming one!?

link   read 7 | post
www.publicspace.ca/postering.htm
www.illegalsigns.ca

lacklusterlulu 12-03 03:57
In my town street cleaners go around with razor sharp spatulas and scrape posters off hydro poles. Gotta keep the streets clean and free of community info that might pollute or corrupt impressionable minds!

earthbound01 12-03 14:21
I think they – the big idjits – don't like postering cuz the corruptrate power monsters have started using it to act all grassrootsy and cuddly (har-har, like they fooled us wily critters!). Another example of the big guys stomping on the little guys. Meanies.

altalake 12-04 22:22
Sarah Harmer and her rockin + rollin friends had a sick benefit concert to fight the anti-postering poopheads. She is one cool chick and as beautiful as her music.

Despite the ostracism (if that's even a real word/ostrichacism?) caused by my at-school and at-home eco-heroics, or maybe because of it, I decided to take my fight to the street. The real streets of the big city.

My new subversive action attack? To fight the silly anti-postering by-law by...postering! Pretty clever, I thought when the idea came to me in a flash as I showered. Funny how a torrent of hot water and some cruelty-free soap gets the inspirational taps flowing.

Plus it would be an excellent togetherness activity for me and my incredibly fantastic boyfriend. The right mix of quasi-radical, middle finger skyward political statement and romantic jaunt about town. It gave me goosebumps to picture it. Vray and me, sticky hand in hand in glue pot in brush on hydro pole. Bummer I hadn't thought of it sooner since the balmy, early wintermission had ended and it was now freakishly chilly.

I just wasn't sure what my poster should say. But I did know that I planned to strategically and ever-so-neatly deface the rows of big glossy album, megamovie and shoe adverts plastered on construction hoarding everywhere. And with the explosion of humungous condo buildings on every single street corner and formerly empty dandelion-infested lot in downtown, there were lots of construction fences to contend with.

The point was, this abuse of power by the corporate monoliths was ruining the artistry and guess-what-dude ethos of the posters put on lamp posts and hydro poles by the staplegun-packing, glue-toting little guys. The posters for yogalates classes and big-hearted movers and little lost doggies and neighborhood garage sales and up-and-coming bands with inventive names and no advertising budgets. The real grassrootsy stuff of our lives.

Finally, after a conversation with, of all people, my dad, I came up with STEAL THIS SPACE. To throw him off the scent, I pretended it was for a school project about urban planning.

Anyway, the words were a modern update on some seventies slogan and book title, *Steal This Book*, which I didn't quite understand since if people stole your book it would be pretty difficult to make a living as a writer (something I imagine isn't easy in the first place). Then again, I suppose that must not have been the point. Or I just missed the point because it was so very clever and subversive and my sophistication radar was not yet so highly attuned.

Needless to say, after some dexterous photoshopping and font sizing and resizing, my poster was done. Well, 8 1/2 x 11 flyer-poster in black on fluorescent green 70% recycled paper. And I was amped!

"Where's the glue bucket," Vray asked as we chose our first target, these big shiny posters announcing U2's album and upcoming tour lined up row after tidy row along a wooden construction fence.

I like to think Bono would approve, given his efforts to make all things equal for as many people as possible. I mean clearly the mucky-muck marketing people didn't ask the BIGGEST BAND IN THE WORLD if they could cheap out and do clandestine quasi-illegal advertising that cannibalized all the space from the LITTLE GUY. Or could they have?

It didn't matter. It was an ideal target. And we were standing right there!

"I brought these." I handed him a yellow sponge-tipped pot scrubber with a hollow handle pilfered from Mom's under-sink collection of about a thousand (for a lifetime of manual dishwashing despite our constant use of the dishwasher). Clever bee that is me, I had filled them with wallpaper paste where the dish soap would normally be.

"It's um, inventive, Bean, but it'll only last for like a dozen posters," Vray said, looking like he'd never seen a clear-handled dishsoap-dispenser sponge in his entire life.

"That's why I brought a whole bunch," I smiled, opening my pack to flash the Tupperware container packed full of them.

"A bucket of paste and a paintbrush would have done the same," he sighed. "These will just end up in landfill when we finish."

I felt a little sick. I hadn't thought of that when I was being an inventive creative genius. Dum-dum me.

"It's not like I went out and got them," I explained. "They were just under the sink begging to be used."

"All right," he said, looking around and grabbing a fistful of flyers from his orange courier bag. "Let's fuck up the man!"

About a half-hour and many dozens of STEAL THIS SPACE mounted flyers later, we were like a couple of giddy teenagers. The fact that we were in fact a couple of giddy teenagers might have had something to do with it, but I couldn't believe how much fun it was to do something that was making a statement and quite possibly a difference! How visceral and exciting it was to actually be out here getting our mitts dirty.

We walked along for a few blocks holding mittened hands, sussing out our next target and just being crazy happy. Then suddenly I had another one of those out-of-body Meta moments where I wondered what we must look like to the people who saw us.

Did we look intense, committed (to each other and other important things) and meaning business? Or maybe just young, silly, carefree and maybe even in love.

"This was an awesome idea, Bean," Vray said as he grabbed me by the waist and pulled my hip up tight against his. "Culture jamming, very cutting edge."

"Frustration does that, I guess," I said, trying to explain why I was motivated to do something about what was going on in the world and not just complain. Not that I needed to because he of all people understood.

"Sexual frustration?" he asked, coyly turning me to face him and pulling my body hard against his hard body and then kissing, kissing, kissing me.

I was quite breathless when I pulled back from him, smiling and a bit dizzy as I found myself falling into his green gaze again.

"Having fun?" he asked, grinning as our frosty breath lingered in the small space between our faces.

I nodded, figuring it was best not to speak for a minute

in case my tongue was sprained from all the intense exercise.

"Thought so. Me, too!"

"How do you do it? How do you stay so up about everything that's so crappy?" I asked finally. "Every time I think about everything that needs fixing my brain hurts. Most people don't even care."

"Most people do care. They just need to be reminded what's important and that's where we come in."

"You make it sound so easy," I sighed.

"It isn't that hard. Look what we're doing today. You had an idea, a really great idea, so you did something. Pretty easy, really."

"Cause you're already on my side and knew it would be fun. Most people don't want to listen, let alone act. I mean Be Green Day was close to a complete bust unless you count Alexis Shaw putting food in her mouth again."

"Then it was far from a complete bust," he said logically. "Everyone just has to do a little bit. It all counts for something. Like cars, right? They aren't going away, so I just never go in a car alone or I subway, walk or ride my bike instead. It's actually kinda fun when it snows."

"So you have your licence?" I asked, confused that Vray might actually be okay with cars.

"Sure, you never know when you have to drive the getaway car!" he grinned. "Look, walking around feeling guilty all the time is not going to help anyone or change anything. Trick is to walk around and be conscious."

"What do you have to get away from?"

"What?"

"The getaway car."

"You're so literal sometimes," he scoffed. "All I'm saying is cars exist, obviously, and people love them. Hell, I even love some of them if they aren't road pig SUVs or those bastard Hummers. You just have to find your line and stick to it."

"My line keeps moving."

"That's okay," he said. "As long as it's in a direction that helps."

"I am trying to move it that way," I answered. "Does trying count?"

"It all counts, Green Bean," he said, sweeping me up again into one of his mind-blowing hugs and staring right in my eyes. "Everything you do matters. You matter."

He said the last two words really slowly and for a split second it almost felt like he was telling me he loved me. And suddenly everything, even the confusing stuff and the tingly electric-shock smoochy stuff, was starting to make sense.

"Let's go. It's freezing standing around and we've got more work to do," he said, taking my hand again and leading me along the sidewalk.

I totally, completely loved this. This day, this moment, this world, this boy. This absolutely everything.

"What are you doing?" I asked Vray as he stopped suddenly and started gluing a poster to the side of a parking tag dispenser – these nifty green solar-powered boxes that had replaced all the parking meters in the city. Pretty progressive actually and no-muss, no-fuss for parking since they took debit and credit cards so you didn't even need change. My mom thought they were great.

"When they took away the parking meters they took away all the places to lock bikes," he explained as he slopped glue all over the poster.

Then he took a step forward to a No Stopping sign and rattled it.

"See the bolts at the bottom of this? People loosen 'em and you think your bike is locked up safe but then – whoop – out comes the post and goodbye bike." He yanked on the post trying to demonstrate, except the bolts were tight and the sign didn't budge.

"There's a bike rack right there," I said, helpfully pointing out the circle-and-post version that took the place of the missing meters.

"There aren't enough," Vray answered, slapping the glue-sopped poster onto the solar meter box. "Everything is about the almighty car."

"But you just said cars aren't going anywhere."

"Neither are bikes and we all need to coexist," he said as if that explained it all. "It's all about emphasis, and always favoring cars doesn't give the other guys a fighting chance."

"Hey! You over there!" A husky uniformed parking-ticket guy shouted from across the street.

"Let's go," Vray said, casually turning to walk up the block in the other direction.

Across the street, the rent-a-cop was looking back and forth waiting impatiently for a break in traffic. Vray had grabbed my arm and was towing me behind him like a little kid as I looked back over my shoulder toward the ticket guy who kept yelling at us.

"You're defacing municipal property," he shouted. "Get back here."

Vray had started running and by extension I was running, too. He bobbed and weaved deftly around all the people and strollers on the sidewalk. Then he ducked down an alley and I scampered behind him, not quite sure what was happening since it was all happening so fast.

He finally stopped behind a large dumpster that smelled like sour garbage and pee. I plugged my nose as I tried to catch my breath.

"See what I told you about the getaway car," Vray laughed, not even slightly winded. "You never know."

"It's not funny. That was scary."

"C'mon Sabine, it was exciting," he said, brushing my hair off my face. "Got your adrenaline pumping, didn't it?"

"Promise me you won't do that again," I said, practically begging.

"What'd I do?" he asked innocently. "Those meter things are public property, and we're the public."

"Just because I might want to make a statement and make things better doesn't mean I want to end up in jail."

"And I do? Trust me, he's got no power. The guy gives out parking tickets. He's like an office drone without an office. Besides, this is not the kind of thing that they put you in jail for, and mucking up posters was your big idea anyway."

"Oh, what, and you've been in jail?" I asked, not really wanting to hear the answer if it was yes.

"No. I like to think I'm smarter than that."

"Me, too," I answered, hoping that he was, and I was, too.

• • •

"It's not a big deal," Ruby assured me the next afternoon at the co-op. "My ex-boyfriend, back when I thought I was into boys, pulled stunts like that all the time."

"As bad, or worse?" I wondered, needing clarification for just how radical Vray was on the radical index.

"Way, way worse. Like a few years ago we went to a W.T.O. thing in Quebec City and the minute we get there, the brainiac chains himself to the crowd-control barriers."

"What happened?" I asked, amazed at the lengths people would go to to be seen and heard. Vast distances I wasn't quite ready to travel. Yet.

"Nothing. The riot police came over, used bolt cutters and told him to get lost. That's when he decided to swear at them using some pretty impressive French slang and he spent the rest of the conference in jail with a bunch of other protesters. That's where he met Monique and, well, I realized he wasn't for me after all."

"I'm pretty sure Vray is for me," I sighed. "I think that's what's freaking me out."

"That's awesome. I love that feeling," Ruby said, doing a little twirl in the aisle. "Better than drugs. Love's the elixir of life. Wish we could bottle it and give it away to everyone in the world."

"So then I'm not overreacting?"

"I hate that expression," she answered emphatically. "You're not overreacting. You're feeling what you're feeling and it's totally fine."

It was a huge relief to have Ruby support me when I really needed someone to talk to and make sure I wasn't crazy. Even if Carmen and Ella had still been in my life, this probably wouldn't have been the kind of thing I'd want to discuss with them.

Not that I expected Ruby to fill the somewhat gaping friendship void. I mean, she was twenty-two and going to art school and had a whole other life going on. She wouldn't want to pal around with some sixteen-year-old activist-in-training.

It's just that she was funny and calm and wise. Sort of like the big sister I never had. Plus she actually listened to me and talked to me like she sincerely cared and understood what I was going through.

"That's so like Matt to flirt with controversy but keep his hands clean," Ruby laughed as she restocked a row of herbal teas. "Sometimes he's such a dilettante."

"Matt? Who's Matt?"

"Matthew Rudolph, dolly, your boyfriend? Please tell me you didn't really think his name was Vray Foret?"

"Well, no. I just never really bugged him about it. He said he changed it formally."

"Smart girl. It's probably a big reason he's so into you. You don't razz him about his big establishment roots."

"You mean his mom and dad? I haven't met them yet, but they sound normal enough. He told me they teach at the university," I said, trying to sound in the know, even though I was clearly not terribly in the know.

"You mean his dad *runs* the university. He's the president and his mom is an extreme scholar, plus Daniel's already in the Ph.D program and he's like only twenty-one or something, major genius."

"I didn't realize you knew him so well." I felt oddly left out and a little stab of jealousy to boot.

"I used to babysit for him. Our parents have been friends forever. I remember when he wore his private school blazer on weekends because he thought it was cool, the dork. But don't tell him I told you."

"So, you think he's okay? I mean, Vray, Matthew, my boyfriend?"

"He's way beyond okay," Ruby laughed, giving me a friendly rub on the shoulder. "If I were younger and boys were my game, I'd be all over him."

"I know, I can hardly keep my hands off him," I giggled. "Or my mind, for that matter."

"He's a good one, Sabine," she said. "A bit unpredictable, but who isn't?"

She was right. I mean, look at what happened with Carmen and Ella who I've only known for forever. And so what if Vray was a bit unpredictable. Unpredictable was just another version of surprising. And surprising was intriguing. And intriguing kept you on your toes and made things interesting.

And I was definitely in the market for more interesting.

A lot more.

e a r t h g i r l
[Dec. 12th | 03:03pm]
[mood | sigh inducing]
[music | warm | kinnie star]

Today my loyal and loverly friends, I give you something a little bit different. A brief survey of the holi-DAZE that is/are fast approaching.

(a) I love all holidays without prejudice.
(b) Holidays suck.
(c) Enforced fun and frolic is neither.
(d) Every day is a celebration.
(e) All of the above.

link   read 8 | post

Vague-a-bond 12-12 16:14
That was way too easy. The answer is of course Zzzzzzzzzz!!!

onederful 12-12 07:53
I was torn between A and B. However, as an eternal optimist, I must choose D. Now please pass that half-FULL glass of eggnog and let's toast to a grand old time.

altalake 12-13 01:01
The universal truth and beauty of holidays and celebrations is that even if they differ from culture to culture, country to country, planet to planet, universe to universe, one thing

earthgirl   138

remains – everyone everywhere has 'em. And someone somewhere hates 'em. Or loves 'em. And I'll always take toast over eggnog.

twelve_

As per tradition, the Solomon clan was bracing for the holiday onslaught by running away from it. Not a bad plan all things considered. This year our happy nuclear family intended to embrace the freakishly freezing weather by skiing in the Eastern Townships outside Montreal.

Normally I'd be pumped but Clare and my parentals had been so grating lately, I wasn't exactly thrilled at the prospect of us all squished in a hotel room doing the 24/7 thing. Plus Dad snored like a bulldozer.

There were also my new concerns about acceptable activities for an eco-conscientious person. On the one hand, some environmentalists and First Nations folks took issue with the very concept of ski resorts. Like the gang who burned down the chairlift and chalet in Colorado or had a bugaboo or two with people using the Cayoosh in B.C. On the other, ski trails provided excellent black bear habitats and allowed people unprecedented access to the great outdoors, which belonged to everyone. It posed yet another quandary, as almost every choice or decision that popped into my path and life seemed to be lately.

Geez, was anything straightforward and easy anymore?

So after many heated closed and open door discussions between the units, I bailed, drooling at having the house entirely to myself for the very first time in my life. And yes, I am not ashamed to admit, thinking naughty thoughts of not being very by myself at all!

"What's Vray's family doing for the holidays?" Mom asked after I'd negotiated my way through another of her carnivorous dinner extravaganzas.

"Cuba," I answered. "His mom's got some conference."

"Sounds smart," Dad said. "Throwing in a holiday and legitimate tax write-off. Nice work if you can get it."

"I don't think that's why," I answered. "She's a mucky-muck economist or something."

"Vray must be excited," Mom said. "He's a musician, right? There's a thriving music community in Havana. Lucky him."

"Yup," I nodded, purposely not mentioning that Vray had opted out of the trip days ago. The awesome creature that was him.

"Thanks for staying for me," I joked without joking when he shared the news. "Risking frostbite over sunburn is extremely romantic."

"You and the band," he answered quickly. "We couldn't pass on a chance to play between Christmas and New Year's. Not that I buy into organized religion and all that ritual shit."

"So you don't celebrate Christmas?" I asked, seeing a chance to learn more about his spiritual perspective and also wondering how to contend with the whole holiday giftie thing if he hated holidays.

"Nope, I've got nothing against other faiths, except for all the dissension and grief they've caused for millennia. Mostly I'm for simple faith in humanity. Don't get me wrong. I'm happy to party on other people's holidays. Why not soak up some cultural karma where you can get it?"

Indeed! This was going to be the best holiday ever! The gig meant he was now going to be around for the entire break and so was I. And, ultra-bonus, there weren't going to be any parents! Or snooping sisters! Or parents!

I was one lucky earthgirl. And Vray Forest, unbeknownst to him, was going to be a very lucky earthboy to boot!

e a r t h g i r l
[Dec. 17th | 07:21pm]
[mood | jolly]
[music | maria | kathleen edwards]

Today I'm very pleased to present my holiday gift to you, my beloved pals and fellow procrastinators, a most excellent list of giftie suggestions for all your holiday (and everyday) gift giving NEEDS:

Love.
    Affection.
        Happy Thoughts.
            Conscious Living.
                Hugs and...Never Ending Smiles!

Happy holidays lovies!!! See you next year! (Love saying that!)

My own holiday gifties were a moderate to substantial success. Even though morally and ethically I was against the fervent consumer sentiment associated with holidays and the extreme pressure to buy bigger, better and more and MORE, I did appreciate that togetherness (when limited to dinner and a movie) and a small token of affection went a long way, too. Never underestimate the power of being thoughtful, I say.

As per my annual Channukah routine, Grammy Sophie got an excellent flowering plant, which she adored. She was always hard to get things for because she had enough picture frames to launch a business and, aside from me, was the biggest anti-consumer-type in the family (go Grams!).

"I have enough, Sabine," she'd say, waving her arms around her cluttered apartment. "A lifetime's worth. What do I need with more things I'm just going to eventually give away or leave behind?"

For Dad I got a fabulous hemp golf shirt and recharge-able batteries, both useful, yet not the kind of thing one buys for themself. Mom let out a little sniff when she saw her eco-cleaning kit complete with nontoxic nonchemical cleaners but squealed when she saw the gorgeous all-organic cotton waffle bathrobe.

"It's just like the ones at the Sunshine Spa!" she giggled as she kissed me on the hair.

"What's in it?" Claire demanded as she tore through my cleverly recycled newspaper comics wrapping paper to reveal the stylin' rubber tire pouch I'd found for her. "It weighs a ton!"

"Nothing," I answered. "It's just the purse."

"Oh," she sighed, looking into the black emptiness and finding the shiny penny I'd left there for good luck. "It looks like a tire."

"It is a tire! Recycled. Pretty clever huh?"

"No," Clare muttered. Then again she was like that about every gift. Even the gift certificates Mom and Dad usually opted for so she wouldn't whine that they didn't understand her or know who she really was.

As for me, I scored a Patagonia shell after many explanations of the company's ethical mandate and quality, some quiet pleading (okay, begging) and not-so-casual around-the-house brochure placement.

All in all a successful haul for our supposed holiday ambivalence.

"You absolutely sure you don't want to come skiing?" Dad asked in a last-ditch effort to twist my arm into forced family frolic.

"Yep," I said twirling around in my excellent new jacket.

"No fair," Clare wailed. "How come she gets Patagucci and I get the no-name special? She doesn't even care about labels and I do."

"Your sister doesn't grow out of things every week. Sabine, you can still reconsider and put that jacket to good use," Mom said. "You can take a black diamond clinic if you think skiing with us is too boring."

"Nope," I said as I took off my fab new winter wear.

"I worry you'll be bored here," Mom sighed. "And lonely."

"I've got lots of shifts at the co-op," I assured. "I'll be fine."

"We appreciate you've got a part-time job," Dad said. "But working through the holidays isn't much of one."

"Oh, like she'll be working," Clare scoffed.

I almost shot her the evil-eye, but realized it would be better to ignore her.

"It's just a few days," I reminded them. "And I'm excited to be on my own for once. I mean, hanging with my friends."

Clare snorted. She was clearly way more on the ball than my parentals. Little creep.

To avoid further interrogation or attempts at guilting, I kissed the units and thanked them again for the choice graft before bolting for my room. Enough with the family stuff already. I wanted to focus my energy and attention on Vray.

Even though he said he didn't care about ritualized holidays, I still wanted to get him a present. I struggled for something meaningful but not too full of meaning. I worried about a gift that made too much of a statement. At the same time, I worried I might end up getting one that didn't say enough. It was a major league tangle for sure.

Before I freaked myself out too much, I decided to enlist Ruby's expertise because (a) she was very fashionable (especially for someone so crunchy and granola, but then she was an art student!) and (b) as a long-time family friend had historical insights into My Guy and (c) she actually had the insight and generosity to offer.

On her very sage advice, I ended up buying him this

beautiful leather lace with a bone amulet on it. It was shaped like a strange letter and the guy in the shop told me it was an Australian aboriginal symbol. Ruby liked it because it looked like the Hindu *Om*, which she explained signified the great power of the other and was chanted before yoga and meditation because the tone had a relaxing, mind and body calming quality.

It was an excellent guy gift. Plus it was international and obscure with a hint of surfer dude, rockstar and tree hugger all rolled into something he could wear around his neck and close to his heart.

But the real present was... me!

Yep, I'd decided that the time was right, the guy was right, all was right in the universe.

That everything had conspired to make this very moment the right one.

thirteen_

The front door was unlocked, so I let myself into Vray's family's old Victorian house. It was this amazing hundred-year-old red-brick place in Cabbagetown, the oldest neighborhood in the city.

I'd already knocked and rung the bell so when he didn't answer after a few long minutes, I tried the brass doorknob. I figured since he was expecting me, he must be home. He probably had on headphones or was in the shower, which also explained why he'd left the door open for me. Very thoughtful, really.

Inside the place was stunning and unlike any of the sub-urbany houses, townhouses or apartments my other friends lived in. The windows were cut glass divided up by black strips, and the late afternoon sun threw these incredible rainbow slices of light on the taupe walls. The ceilings were high and the dark wood floors were shiny where they weren't covered in beautiful, exotic-looking rugs. Everything besides the kitchen, which definitely belonged in a movie or on a cooking show with its sparkling pots hanging above the huge restaurant stove, seemed like it had lived a dozen life-times before it ended up there.

I was so excited I practically raced up the narrow creaky staircase to his room on the third floor. But since I didn't want to be all winded when I got there, I slowed down near the top.

Vray's door was ajar and I could hear the lowing sounds of Thom Yorke's squeaky strange voice in the background. I never quite got Radiohead. I could barely understand what they were singing, even if I liked their politics.

I took a long deep breath and tried to calm the crazy smile that was exploding off my face and filling up my entire body at what was about to happen! My boyfriend and me consummating our love for each other and the world. What a funny word, consummating! Combo of consuming and mating, har har!

I was practically bouncing off the walls as I stepped through the door and saw him.

He was lying propped up in his messy bed with his arm in a navy canvas sling like a broken puppet. His cheek had the pale, yellowish hue of a bruise in progress. It looked like he'd been jumped and clobbered. Swarmed.

"Hey babe," he slurred when he saw me. His eyes were glassy and he looked completely spaced out.

"What happened?" I asked as I darted toward him, wanting to hold him and kiss his damp face, but frightened I might break him more than he already appeared to be broken.

"Busted my collarbone," he sighed. "Hurts like a bastard so I'm hopped up on painkillers, which I'd like to point out live up to their name."

"How? What happened?"

"Some MoFo Navigator who couldn't navigate squeezed me out," he snorted with a drowsy drawl.

"Didn't he see you?"

"Obviously not," he half laughed, lifting the sling an inch before clenching his teeth and wincing in pain.

"And he didn't even stop? That's hit and run!" I was shocked and horrified as my mind raced at what could have happened to poor Vray.

To my Vray.

"Oh, he stopped. Had to inspect the damage to his pig-mobile. Too bad there wasn't any. Then, get this, creep has the nerve to say I shouldn't ride my bike in the winter, like it's any of his fucking business. Jerk-off."

"Did the police come? Did they charge him with danger-ous driving? Nail his ass to the wall?"

"You know, you're pretty cute when you get all worked up," Vray laughed, patting the damp pillow beside him. "I think he got a ticket for an improper lane change or some-thing, like he cares."

I sat carefully beside him, brushing the sweat-knotted hair off his forehead and kissing his unbruised cheek. I looked at my broken boyfriend and even though I didn't want to be selfish, I couldn't help feeling disappointed and even angry that this had happened. At this supposed-to-be epic moment.

He couldn't even hug me and I might hurt him if I touched him.

"Are your parents coming back?" I asked, suddenly real-izing the other implications of this horrible accident.

"Nah," he sighed. "I'll be okay in a coupla days. My dad dispatched his sister Martha to make sure I've got food and don't OD on meds or something, but she's cool."

"What about the band? The Christmas show?"

"Don't remind me," he groaned.

"Well, at least you can still sing," I offered, even though his thrashy guitar was actually the best thing about his singing.

"I don't want to think about any of that right now." He let out a breath that sounded like he was deflating.

"I can't believe you got hurt," I said, snuggling gently up to his good shoulder. And how much it hurt me to see him lying there like that. All mangled and broken and beaten down.

"It's a collarbone, Green Bean. Most commonly broken bone in the body, but hurts like a MoFo, I'll tell you that much."

"This is awful. I'm so sorry this happened," I said as I ran my hand through his curls.

I'm so sorry this happened to you. To me. To us.

"Finn nearly got his eye taken out by some asswipe waving a cigarette out the window last summer. Should've seen the scratch he left on the dude's Lexus. Priceless," Vray said with a glint in his eye.

"He scratched his car?"

"Not intentionally, unfortunately, and it was the guy's fault anyway. He pulls over in the No Stopping bike lane like a pompous jerk. So Finn's riding in front of me and pulls out to pass him when this fat, pasty arm shoots out the driver's window and nails Finn with a lit butt. Finn's so freaked he swerves, but there's cars beside us and he ends up scraping against the guy's fender, *ccccccrrrrrrrssssskkkk*. It was a beautiful thing."

Even though I was sort of shocked at the way Vray described it, I was also a little pumped. And almost sorry I hadn't done some of my own scratch-worthy damage to the littering lunatic lady's car.

At the very moment, I hated drivers and especially those arrogant S.U.X. drivers with every cell of my being. I hadn't exactly liked them and their obnoxious oversized steroid-fed cars before, but that didn't compare with the anger and disgust I was feeling right now.

Before this moment, it had been an abstract kind of anger at what they stood for and were doing to the planet. How they drove around in their monster machines as if their lives depended on it. Like it was their right.

Now their greed and gluttony had had a direct impact on me and my life. Their choices and actions affected me, my boyfriend, my life and my plans.

It was outrageous.

"We should do something," I said. "When you're better, we should do something major. I mean, what's with these people? First that crazy woman hurls her garbage at me and now this! It's like some kind of four-wheel conspiracy to kill and maim cyclists! We have to do something."

"Man, you're hot when you're all amped up like that," Vray said quietly. "Sucks that I can't do much about it. Can't even wrap my arms around you and slobber all over your hot little bod. Well, just my one arm, but I wish it were both."

Me, too, I thought, letting out a sigh and snuggling carefully against his chest.

• • •

We must have fallen asleep because it was Vray's Aunt Martha who woke us a while later.

"Hey, there, Matty, looks like you're feeling a bit better," Martha said, giving us both a gentle nudge.

"Painkillers," Vray answered sleepily. "And I asked you to please not call me that."

"Roger that, Vray. Hi, I'm Martha, his amazing aunt, and you must be the fabulous Sabine," she said, turning to me with a big smile and the same sparkling green eyes as Vray. "At least I hope so, or I'm going to be more embarrassed than either of you at this particular second."

"Who else would she be?" Vray snorted.

"Yes," I nodded as I scooched up from the pillow, wiping away the grotty film of sleep from my mouth. "And I was just leaving." Not to mention epically embarrassed to have been caught like that, even if she was very sweet about it.

"Don't even think about it," she said nonchalantly. "If you stay here tonight I can go home. You're good to stay over, right?"

I didn't know what to say. I'd never met an adult who was so casual in a situation like this. Even if it did involve a sensible girl and a dosed-up, busted and groggy boy.

"She can hang out and play nurse," Vray answered for me. "We were talking about it right before you got here."

"Great. It's about time Matty — sorry, Vray — had more positive female energy in his world," Martha smiled as she swept across the room briskly tidying things up like a jeans-and fleece-wearing Mary Poppins. "Nice contrast from that pack of wolves he usually runs with."

"Grrrr," Vray growled at her.

"I've got pizza and salad in the kitchen. You can get your sorry butt downstairs out of this manky room to eat something, right?" she said as she bounded out the door onto the landing.

"Did she just ask me to sleep over?" I looked at Vray.

"Yup," Vray grinned wickedly.

"To sleep over here with you, alone?"

"Oh, like you hadn't planned to?" he said, pointing to my bulging backpack on the floor beside one of his many teetering towers of smartypants books.

"You knew?" I asked, feeling vaguely thrilled he was so clued in. So in tune with me and what was on my mind.

"Sort of," he answered, his glassy eyes sparkling and nodding toward an unopened box of condoms tucked beside the night-table lamp. "I definitely hoped so. If not tonight sometime during the holidays."

"I can't believe I'm so transparent," I said, leaping off the bed to smooth my hair and unrumple my clothes. "I might even be insulted."

"Why? We're just totally in sync," he said softly.

"We are, aren't we," I agreed, with another one of those overwhelming body-engulfing smiles taking me over. "Like two of a kind."

"No, more than that," he said. "Almost like you're the other half of me, if that even makes sense."

I took a deep breath and held myself steady. It was almost more than I could bear, hearing him say the very things I was feeling. Saying the words that made those very feelings true.

Absolutely, totally, completely true.

• • •

That night, in his bed, in the dark, we did things I'd never done before. Things I'd only read about or talked about or imagined. It was totally unexpected when he unspooned himself from me and with his good arm nudged my body toward him and started tracing and touching me in ways I'd never been touched. With his fingers and his toes, his eyelashes and his mouth, his hands and his heart. He whispered things and sighed and asked and explained. And I did the same in return.

It was calm and intense. Quiet and yet cacophonous like a sudden thunderstorm tearing through a humid summer night and then suddenly gone as quickly as it appeared.

Because of his limited mobility and my anxiety that I'd hurt him, we weren't totally intimate, but I have to say it was still extremely intimate. It wasn't everything, but it was almost more.

And afterwards, even though I didn't sleep a second, as I watched him lie there supported by a stack of pillows, breathing noisily, I'd never felt more awake in my life.

Everything was amazing. The jagged outline of frost on the edges of the window. The sour-sweet heat of his breath

on my neck and shoulder. Even the way he sprawled diago-
nally across the bed, barely giving me any room or sharing
the duvet was wonderful.

"How's you?" he asked sleepily as the gray morning light
filled the room.

"Fine. Pretty tired, but amazingly fine," I said, turning
my head and covering my mouth to spare him my jungle
breath. "How are you? Is your shoulder okay?"

"No, it sucks," he half laughed, reaching past the
untouched toy box for another painkiller and a sip of water.

"Watch it with those things," I cautioned. "They're pretty powerful."

"I know," he said, his eyes widening a bit. "I had the
wildest dream. All this soft gorgeous naked skin and hair
and wow. It was so real, it's getting me all, um, you know,
just thinking about it." He didn't have to explain himself
since it was quite obvious as he got up from the bed and tot-
tered slowly to the bathroom.

"I had the same dream, too," I called softly behind him.
"Funny thing is I wasn't asleep."

When he returned he handed me the glass of water he'd
refilled and climbed back in beside me. I took a long cold
sip, amazed that I could be lying here on the duvet-covered
bed of this messy, stinky boy room beside such an amazing
creature.

"It's funny. You know so much about me, and I sometimes feel like I barely know anything about you," I said. "I
mean, do I even know your real name."

"Sure you do. I told you that day we met."

"No, your real, real name."

"I don't have a name or a label or a barcode," he sighed, leaning forward to kiss me again. "I only have this mind and this body and this amazing moment right now with you."

Then there was another kiss. A warm, wet, sloppy, untoothbrushed hypnotic kiss. Anything else he said at that point was like the roar of a jet overhead. The breathless crashing of the ocean against a rocky beach. An epic, supernatural, sonic swoosh. And a warm, completely comfortable and safe feeling like the greatest hug on earth.

Love and kisses were the absolutely best thing ever! Better than fresh raspberries. Better than just-baked chocolate chip cookies. Maybe even better than fresh air and wild dolphins and blue-black starry nights and snow-covered mountains.

Or at the very least just as great!

Yup, even if the world was in crisis, choking and struggling amidst the crap we were foisting on it, this moment was transcendent.

Because where there's love, there's hope. And that made me certain there was something we could do. Had to do.

fourteen_

After two seriously long days and nights of no sleep, I was severely exhausted and a tad grumpy. This despite the extreme dreamy bliss of Vray's companionship and cuddleship. With my few awake and operational brain cells, I realized I had to get home and into my own bed for some major-league zzzzz's. And rather soonish, too.

Part of me wanted to stay at Vray's for every single solitary second possible. I even flirted with the idea of calling in sick for one of my co-op shifts to snuggle for a few more hours. Who could blame me, really? I'd never ever shared a bed with a boy before, so even if it left me sleep deprived and punchy, it seemed worth the sacrifice.

Another part of me could barely think or sit up or consider another trip up and down the three flights of stairs between his room and the kitchen. Then there was the annoying fact that after our first night together, it seemed like we were never alone again.

I don't even remember Vray inviting them, but it seemed like Finn and Eric were at his house for the entire time, too, practically inhaling every last crumb of food that Aunt Martha had thoughtfully left in the fridge.

Don't get me wrong. I was happy to be with my guy, even if I did have to share him. And at times it was very exciting, not to mention enlightening, to be around such feisty and politicized guys. But it was also incredibly tiring. For socially conscious world-aware green-beings, there sure was a whole lot of boy energy hogging the room. Not to mention hogging my boy's attention.

Like when they spent what seemed like three hours riffing on possible song lyrics and potential fantasy gigs for O-Zone.

"Definitely Linkin Park," Vray announced. "We open for them, we're set for life."

"As long as it's not on the downslide or some lame reunion tour," Eric scoffed. "We gotta make it happen soon."

"Yeah," Finn agreed, looking soulful and moony like he could actually see them on stage in front of that many people at some point in the near (let alone far) future.

Maybe I was missing something, but I found it hard to even imagine a full club of people coming to see them for a free gig. But if you're going to have dreams, they may as well be big, right?

"Me, I'd bring back that vulvapalooza tour," Eric said. "All the little hotties with those low back tattoos. Yum, it would be like a buffet."

"It's called the Lilith Fair and the point of those concerts was to showcase female artists," I said.

"Exactly, and times are a-changing with babes or babe-fronted groups all over the charts, so if they did a retro-tour, they should put a trip like us on the bill to help us break large," Eric answered. "We should write a song about it – a protest song demanding equality."

Sometime during this particularly infantile conversation, it was also decided that even if they couldn't find a sub, the Christmas Eve gig would go ahead minus Vray's guitar. Even though I could hardly picture Vray tearing up the stage in a sling, it somehow seemed like the sanest thing they had actually said in hours.

I was hoping the guys might decide to leave after that so we could be alone again, but no such luck.

After the exhaustive and exhausting discussion about their musical delusions and aspirations, they spent something like three days debating the merits of tree planting in northern Ontario and Quebec versus heading out to British Columbia. At one point Eric raved about Bella Coola and Bella Bella, where some guy he'd met at a logging protest ran a crew.

"The dude was a major highballer so he always gets the run of the cream," Eric waxed on.

"Hello?" I waved. "Tree-planting virgin here. Same language, please?"

"So there are virgins in the room," Eric smirked. "As suspected."

I pretended I didn't hear him. Or care. And tried to will myself to not turn pink.

"He means the guy planted the most trees at the camp so he gets a nice clean block of land to plant," Finn explained when Eric stopped yammering long enough to take a gulp of beer.

I definitely preferred Finn to Eric, who was a bit raw and a lot rude. Not that it mattered since my taste was for Vray Foret and he was already on my menu and hopefully daily diet!

If Vray hadn't been mangled and medicated, I might have been miffed he didn't steer his buddies to include me more. Not that I needed him to stand up for me, but just to point out that I was there and important to him. Clearly I'd have to force the issue or suck it up. And since fatigue was the deciding factor, I closed my eyes, tuned them out and tried to have a mini-disco nap against Vray's uninjured shoulder.

It didn't exactly work. It was "Bella this" and "Bella that," followed by "slashes and stashes and screefs and duffs." At one point I thought they were making up words just to confuse me until I later checked the map and realized the two Bellas actually did exist. And treeplanters do have their own vernacular.

It was already dark outside and yet Eric and Finn showed no signs of having anywhere else to go. Didn't they have other friends? Or families?

I tried to stay Zen and relaxed. I didn't want Vray to think I was jealous and possessive. Or that I didn't adore hanging with his buddies as much as he seemed to.

So I ate lentil soup and crackers while they spent what seemed like the next three weeks arguing about the proliferation of "agroceuticals and genetically modified crops" that were going to leave subsequent generations with extra limbs and strange stupid superpowers like the ability to lick your own earlobes.

It was downright random and ridiculous at times. Sure they cussed and swore for a minute when Vray told them about being run off the road, but they didn't seem remotely interested in an intelligent discussion about how we could protest or possibly even retaliate despite my best efforts.

"We should join the Cycling Committee to demand more bike lanes," I suggested.

"Get a load of Sabine," Eric said. "Five hits on her YouTube bitchslap and she's the authority on activism."

"I never said that," I answered, wondering why my boyfriend wasn't defending me and hoping it was just him being tired and injured. "I just don't think we can assume things will happen without making some noise."

"Slashing tires is more effective," Vray said, mussing up my hair with his good arm. "And I happened to enjoy the bitchslap."

"I'm serious," I continued, wondering if that was his version of standing up for me. "They have those Critical Mass rides once a month to promote bikes. You know, hordes of people on bikes slowing down traffic, forcing the cars to make room for us. To notice and acknowledge our rights."

"If you were really serious, you'd carry a knife," Eric said. "Swiss Army does the trick, and it has a nifty corkscrew."

"Plain old nails work, too," Finn laughed. "Cause a nice slow debilitating leak that doesn't always get noticed right away."

I let out a loud sigh and sank back into the couch. It was exhausting trying to make my point. Plus I was very, very sleepy. And didn't want to risk exhaustion making me sick.

Not with the holidays stretched out in front of me. And the possibility of Vray stretched out beside me to boot!

So, after a long, luxuriating smooch (set to the soundtrack of Finn's whoops and Eric's groans), I set off to my boring empty house.

e a r t h g i r l
[Dec. 22nd | 07:21pm]
[mood | exhausted/angry/frustrated]
[music | battleflag — lo fidelity allstars + dead machines]

The personal is definitely, positively the political! And the political is sometimes very, very personal. Especially when your innocent, lovely, beloved boyfriend gets run down by a crazed S-U-X!!!

The result? His broken collarbone and my broken heart. Fortunately, our spirits are intact. But just barely.

Which leads me to the most excellent anarchist artists known as Action Terroriste Socialement Acceptable — which translates roughly to activist artists making socially acceptable commentaries, but in French is more poetic bien sur (of course).

Attack #9: Oil Kills is a burned out, wrecked and wretched SUV put in public spaces to comment on stupidhead love affairs with stupidhead truckcars.

Eerie. Like they were bombed. Or mangled. And torched. Destroyed in response to their destructiveness. I so totally get their art. It almost makes me feel queasy. In a good uneasy, queasy way!

link   read 5 | post
www.atsa.qc.ca

altalake 12-22 23:58
So the other day – inspired by you earthgirl –
I googled Hummer and these stellar rogue cul-
turejammers pop up. Much hilarity ensues especially from the stupid ass defenses of the
fat-arsed people who drive them and can never
find a big enuf spot to park them. Like we care?
www.fuh2.com

lacklusterlulu 12-23 09:40
according to the WTO, there are over one billion overweight
people in the world. 30% of americans are considered too fat.
and each extra pound in cars uses up more than 39 MILLION
extra gallons of gas. Junk in the Trunk indeed.
I AM NOT MAKING THIS UP!

earthbound01 12.23 14:31
Isnt Hummer a word for Hard-on? Or is that supposed to be the
point? Limp dicks drive 'em cuz its the best they can do? Talk about
auto-erotica!

MachFhive 12-20 0:03
U skinny leaf eating freeks are jealous u don't have muslces and
money. admit it. SUCKAHS.

fifteen_

Whoever thought being with the band was a nonstop thrill-filled glamfest has obviously never been a roadie. Even for one piddly trip between car and venue, and by my count it was seventeen grueling trips each way for this, that and whatever. And with the other guys acting all rockstar, it felt like I was the one doing most of the grunting and hauling.

By the end of the evening, my arms and back seemed almost as battered and bruised as Vray's poor collarbone. With him barely able to carry electrical cables, I volunteered to help set up and tear down the Xmas eve gig. It's one thing to say you're a supportive girlfriend. You have to walk the talk sometimes, even if it includes heavy gear.

Even though it was an opening slot on a night when most normal people were busy, snagging the show was apparently a major coup. The venue was a grungy metal bar on Queen West called the Bovine Sex Club. And as I'd feared, pretty sucky over all. Though not as empty as you might expect on a night like that.

There were lots more people than at the Earth Action League gig by a long shot, though they seemed equally dis-interested in the band or the music or the message. Funny that none of the guys even noticed. As I helped Finn shlep the heavy amp toward his sister's jeep, he kept going off about how tight they were. Eric was in a pretty good mood, too, but still mean and snarky to me. Sorta like the older brother I'd never had and never wanted.

"You better not get us busted for being underage," he kept warning me, so I'd stay away from the bar that stretched the length of the joint. "We lied our asses off to get this show and some little princess isn't going to blow it for us."

"Relax," Vray said, coming to my defense for once. "Sabine's tuned in. Besides, she looks older than we do."

The mature, sophisticated me was totally knocked out by his supportive comment, even if the sixteen-year-old me wanted to stick out my tongue at Eric. He was so smug and annoying. I wasn't really sure why someone as fab as Vray was even friends with him. Obviously I was missing or ignoring something deeper and more significant.

Finn as always was sweet and polite. And Peter the drummer and tallest, skinniest guy I'd ever set eyes on was decent and didn't seem to have a beef with me. I also exchanged a brief nod with Ashok who was filling in for Vray on guitar and seemed nervous about not knowing all the songs. Neither said much, but then it was pretty loud most of the time anyway.

At the end of the gig we had to clear the stage quickly for the next band. I would have been just as happy to stay and hear them, but Eric was in a big hurry to herd us out. We were so stuffed into the jeep with gear that I couldn't see out

165   **earthgirl**

the fogged-up windows. So I was a bit surprised when Finn pulled up in front of my house to drop me off (a) because he remembered where it was from the long-ago fridge fiasco and (b) because I hadn't asked to be let off there.

I peeled myself out of the squishy backseat and Vray walked me to the door.

"Don't you want to come in?" I asked, hoping that all along he'd planned to stay with me here in my house in my very own bedroom and just forgot to mention it.

"Nah, I'm wrecked. I'm gonna crash at home, but I'll see you tomorrow." He leaned in and gave me a speedy kiss. "Thanks a ton for helping and putting up with the guys. You're awesome."

And then he was gone, leaving only a brief memory of his warm mouth on mine and a little puff of frost-filled air.

• • •

"This is leek and mushroom loaf. That's squash and teriyaki grilled tempeh," Ruby explained, waving her hand over the table of vegified wonders that looked and smelled absolutely incredible. "I flirted with doing a tofurkey, but then remembered you mock meat objectors."

"Meat's already a mockery," Vray quipped, his uninjured hand reaching for a steaming casserole dish.

"What's wrong with tofurkey?" I asked as he offered me a scoop of steaming something yum. "Besides the goofy name?"

"If you make the effort to be vegetarian, you shouldn't eat stuff trying to pass itself off as animal carcasses."

It was Boxing Day afternoon and we were in the most

magical place I'd ever been. A little wooden cottage on Algonquin Island, the sparsely populated public parkland across the harbor from downtown Toronto. Ruby and her girlfriend Hayley were housesitting for friends lucky enough to live in this hippy-esque community of two hundred or so houses.

I knew it existed, a short walk from the amusement park on the adjacent Centre Island, but I'd never bothered to check it out before. Too busy munching candyfloss or riding the bumpercars, I guess. Silly, silly me. It was a little piece of paradise a hop, skip, subway and boat ride from home.

To get there, Vray and I took the icebreaker ferry, which ran all year. Even though it was snowing, blowing and seriously freezing, we huddled outside at the bow and watched the heavy metal boat break through the ice-filled channel between the city and the island across the bay.

Small and large chunks of cloud-colored ice were pushed aside from the open-water pathway. It made clinking and crackling and pinging noises like a spring being sprung as we passed through, and I started to wonder what it would be like to be in a frozen world like the Arctic or Antarctica. To be surrounded by sparkling blue ice and pristine snow and silence and whales and polar bears or penguins. Before global warming melts them into memories.

I felt incredibly special and incredibly lucky. There's no way I'd ever have experienced anything like this if I was still the same old boring Sabine Solomon I'd been back in September. A lifetime ago. It had only been a few months and yet I'd met the most extraordinary people and learned the most incredible things.

Ruby and Hayley had invited Vray and me and their friends Tibor, Cassie and Steve, who all looked interesting and arty and socially conscious and at least in their early twenties. I was definitely the baby, but no one seemed to notice. Completely opposite to hanging out with the smug boys. It was totally awesome. An honor, even.

And this feast! Whoever thought vegetables were boring never had a meal cooked by Ruby. I could eat this stuff for the rest of my life.

And it was so much more than that. The conversation was fast and furious, yet intense and meaningful. Exclusive and yet inclusive and endlessly interesting.

"He's chronicling the neo-industrial revolution sweeping the earth," Hayley gushed about the photos of Edward Burtynsky, a world-renowned artist who lived in Toronto. "Essential, in their scale and message."

Apparently, his forte was mega-sized photos of open-pit mines and factories and construction sites. There was even a movie about his photos of China. Tibor had spent a few months working at a photo lab that processed his work.

"Companies give him access to document the way they're raping and pillaging the earth," he explained. "Then spend bags of money to put the art in their corporate collections."

"Is that bad?" I asked. "I mean, they're supporting the artist, right? And besides, isn't old-style photography a kind of contradiction considering all the chemicals used to process it?"

"Yeah," he agreed, making me feel both pride and relief that I actually knew something. "Very astute and something I struggled with when I worked there."

"Take a beautiful picture of a lake, then pour the developer and fix down the drain and it ends up in that pristine lake," Ruby interjected. "That's why I draw and paint, but sadly a lot of art is incredibly toxic. Then again, something has to be worth the risk."

"And rewards," Tibor added with a devilish grin. "You live for the adulation and contempt as much as me. You're too precious to admit it."

"Ignore him. He equates art with immortality," Cassie smiled, waving her long, slender hand which had silver and chunky stone rings on every finger. "Considering his ego, it's a miracle we let him hang out with us at all."

"Ah, but someone has to throw the wrench in the machine, even if it's a progressive machine," Tibor growled, giving her a sloppy kiss on the cheek.

"Actually, Sabine threw that wrench," Vray said.

"I throw a mean caber," Steve added. "But I'm Scottish."

"What's a caber?" I asked, delighted to be in the thick of such a dynamic conversation, not to mention making a contribution.

"It's like a big hydro pole," Hayley said. "And Stevie's never thrown more than a good party or the odd hissy fit as long as we've known him."

"But I do look great in a kilt," Steve boasted.

"I for one need more wine," Tibor sighed, reaching across the table and filling his glass.

Everyone's glasses except mine were filled as he nodded and waved the bottle toward me.

I hedged. I wasn't very experienced with alcohol and didn't want to barf or embarrass Vray.

"It's okay," Ruby assured me. "We won't let you get drunk."

"And not cause you're underage," Cassie chimed in. "Pissed people aren't very interesting."

"Touché," Tibor said a bit loudly before taking a sip and putting his glass back down on the table.

I wondered if maybe he was going to turn into the drunk and uninteresting guest. There was no way I'd let it be me.

"Okay, where were we?" Steve asked.

"The good and bad of making art," Cassie said.

"There's good and bad in everything. Art, life, progress, you name it," Ruby added. "It's all a matter of perspective and action."

"Says the Buddhist Pollyanna," Steve teased.

"If you decide things are bad, they're going to *be* bad, so you might as well decide they're good and do something to make them better," Hayley answered.

"Too late," Vray said. "It's way past the best-before date."

"Totally. We're at the nadir of civilization," Hayley explained, mopping her plate clean with a piece of pita. "Look around. If we're not killing each other, we're killing the planet or it's killing us to retaliate. Something's gotta give."

"Are you saying the world's ending?" I asked, even though it seemed obvious that's exactly what she was saying.

Still, I was kind of confused because even as she ranted, she smiled and laughed and stuffed her face and sipped wine like everything was totally fine.

"Explain the unbelievable disparity between rich and poor, haves and have nots?" Ruby said.

"The wanton destruction of forests, waterways, the civil wars, droughts, crazy weather, global pandemics," Hayley continued, like they were sharing the same brain.

"People are selfish and greedy. Even if they pretend they're not. It's definitely the beginning of the end," Vray agreed, as he motioned for the pan of apple and pear crumble.

"It makes me nutso how selfish people are," Steve said. "As if they deserve whatever they want whenever they want it and, um, hasn't anyone ever heard of holding a door for someone else?"

"Blabbing on cellphones asleep at the wheel," Vray said as he shoveled down another mouthful of food. From the way he was eating you'd think he'd never seen food before, but then I've heard when the body is repairing itself nutrition is very important.

"I totally agree!" Hayley blurted out. "People walk around in little bubbles and tune out everything around them. It's sick."

"I can't even remember what people did before mobiles or MP3 players isolated them from everyone," Steve said softly.

"Pondered the universe, smelled the flowers, lived life," Ruby answered, turning to me. "Hey, how come you've never written about cellphones or iPods in your blog?"

171   **earthgirl**

"Because she's got them," Vray intercepted.

"Only for emergencies," I said.

"Right, an iPod emergency," Vray laughed.

"I got it way before I learned all this," I said, feeling suddenly guilty for all the things I had when other people had so much less. "And I barely use my phone any more except if it's crucial." Since Vray was essentially anti-cellular and there was no need to text Carmen or Ella, I hadn't used it in months. And I hadn't really missed it, either.

"Have you noticed there are barely any pay phones any more? Side effect of the cellular obsession. Not great for public safety or poor people," Steve added.

"They need to be maintained and get vandalized," Tibor said. "The telcos want to hook you on convenience and would rather pour money into cell matrixes that transmit weird frequencies and give us all brain cancer."

"You should write about all this," Ruby said encouragingly. "The earthgirl disses antisocial so-called conveniences. It's a great thread."

"So you're the infamous earthgirl!" Cassie suddenly gushed.

My mouth was full of tempeh, so I smiled madly and nodded like a bobblehead.

"Ruby sent me the link to your page ages ago," Cassie went on as I quickly swallowed my food. "No wonder you look familiar. I can't believe I didn't make the connection right away."

"You've read it? Did you like it?" I asked excitedly, immediately regretting it in case she didn't.

"Like it? I post all the time. I'm Vague-a-bond!" At this point we both jumped up from the table and were spontaneously hugging while the others whooped and cheered.

"I can't believe you're only sixteen. You're so wise and insightful," Cassie said, looking me deep in the eyes. "Definitely an old soul."

"Told you she was awesome," Ruby gushed, like she'd discovered me in a basket on her porch. It was odd to be claimed like that, but also flattering considering the caliber of the crowd.

"Sick stuff on SUVs," Vray said.

"You said blogs were self-indulgent time wasters," I responded, absolutely thrilled he'd been checking out my pages.

"I was curious what you were ranting about," he shrugged.

"Try if you ranted about him," Ruby teased.

"Ahem," Tibor said, clearing his throat. "I don't mean to derail this adorable train of thought, but can we get back to where we were?"

"You absolutely do," Cassie laughed. "Hijacking conversations is your specialty."

"True," Tibor nodded. "So anyway, we were on this end-of-the-world thing, to which I say, screw recycling. It's a crap idea."

"I thought recycling was good," I said, a bit relieved the focus had shifted off me even if I caught Ruby rolling her eyes when Tibor spoke.

"Tibor's a re-evolutionary," Cassie explained. "He thinks

we have to reconfigure society and values to create a better world. Zero waste and all that."

"Definitely," Vray agreed, as if it was the simplest thing in the world.

"Love people and use things," Cassie said knowingly.

"Too bad most people have it backwards," Ruby replied. "They love things and use people instead."

"All our problems are because as a society, Western society, we don't believe in reincarnation," Hayley said softly. "If we did, we'd realize things could go on to other lives, too, instead of death in landfills."

I didn't know what to think. Everything that we had talked and argued and laughed about was all so powerful and insightful and hopeful and depressing at the same time.

Sort of, I guess, the way life could be. The way life should be when you finally woke up and got engaged in the world around you.

• • •

In the flurry of our epic meal and conversation, we missed the last ferry back to the city, stranding us at the cottage. Ruby, Hayley, Tibor, Cassie and Steve were still deep in wine and words when Vray and I stole away to a tiny bedroom at the back of the house.

"What's this?" Vray asked, as I sat on the antique bed and handed him a little brown paper bag tied with a bow.

"Just a little thing, for Christmas or Kwanzaa or Channukah, whatever it is you might celebrate," I said.

"All and none," he answered. "You didn't have to do this."

"I know. I wanted to," I smiled, secretly hoping without hoping that maybe he'd gotten me something, too.

Not that it mattered, since I really didn't need any more things. I didn't want to be one of those people we'd just talked about who loved things instead of people. Loving people should be all that mattered. Especially now.

"I got you something," he said, as if he was reading my mind. "But it's at home and more a New Year thing, anyway."

"You didn't have to," I said, even though I was totally elated that he had.

"I know." He tugged at the hemp string I'd tied around the paperbag wrapping to make it look festive without being wasteful or indulgent or unrecyclable. As he took out the pendant, a massive smile took over his face.

"It's awesome."

"I loved it when I saw it, I mean *liked* cause it seemed perfect for you and it's a thing and you don't love things, right?" I knew I was rambling, but I couldn't help it since I knew deep, deep down that this was a very big moment and I wanted to keep it alive as long as I could.

"No, not things, just people." And then he took my face in his hands and looked me in the eye. He was staring at me with a serious, unflinching stare. Staring me down almost like a challenge. "And," he said with a big, long, breathy pause as he leaned in toward me, "I love you."

"I love you, too," I sighed a second later as I came up for air. To breathe in his breath and his scent and his words and this the most incredible moment in my lifetime EVER!

But no matter how amazing it was, no matter how astonishing and uber and unprecedented, my brain was still buzzing from all the things we'd discussed that night. All the good, bad and ugly of people and the planet. It was something I somehow couldn't shake.

"Do you really, truly think the world is ending?" I asked Vray a few minutes later as I crawled under the duvet.

"Not this minute," he said, getting in beside me and spooning me against him.

"In our lifetimes?"

"Anything's possible," he said with a yawn.

"So then it could end? We could destroy it all?"

"Anything's possible means we could also turn it around if we do the right things," he mumbled into my neck.

"What things?" I asked turning to face him.

"Sabine, I'm wrecked," he sighed. "Can we pick this up tomorrow?"

I nodded in the dark, hugged his arm around my shoulder and closed my eyes.

• • •

And it was in the sleepy depths of the night, in the soft warmth of the strange old bed, that I gave Vray my body. My natural, oatmeal-bar buffed, almost-vegetarian body. I have to say I was somewhat surprised given his still brokenness and the strangeness of where we were. Not so surprised that we didn't play it safe and smart, but it was still sort of unexpected given the venue.

Even if it was the next logical step in my evolution as the earthgirl. As the earthWOMAN, I thought. I'd already given him my soul and devotion.

It was nice. Not mind-blowing like I'd expected, given all the hype. More awkward and goofy and giggly than movie romantic. The sex part anyway. Though that could have had something to do with my huge self-consciousness at being in someone else's house and bed. Something that Vray didn't seem to care about in the least! Boys.

And honestly, when it came down to it, not all that much better or more exciting or intense than the gropey and kissy stuff we'd already managed to do. In his bed, in his house. Then again, his still-limited mobility was probably a factor, too. Plus my own nervousness considering people were in the rooms next door!

One thing I did positively for sure know. I felt incredibly strong and powerful and motivated and loved. And for the first time in my life, I felt important.

Significant.

Like what I thought and said and felt and did could make a difference. Would make a difference. However small.

e a r t h g i r l
[Dec. 31st | 03:33pm]
[mood | HAPPY HAPPY HAPPY]
[music | bif naked — that's life]

In the waiting room at my dad's office, there's a whack o' crap magazines and oddly enuf a little book of ZEN sayings. one of his favorites is: "When you can do nothing, what can you do." (Now imagine it in a bland dad tone of voice.)

It's obviously supposed to mean relax and chill and dont worry. To take things as they come and blabity-blah-blah.

Well, I think it SUCKS!!!!!

I truly believe that we can always do SOMETHING, or at the very least TRY. However big or little. Actions make ripples that resonate around the world.

So instead of making silly old New Year's resolutions that will end up in the toilet or the landfill or somewhere useless – make your ripple today!

"When you can do nothing, you really should be doing SOMETHING!"

link   read 5 | post
www.earthonempty.com

onederful 01-01 10:12
Happy New You and may all your ripples make waves!!!!

altalake 01-01 01:01
turns out feeding and handling a cow for one hamburger creates as much greenhouse gas as a 10 km car ride! The Union of Concerned Scientists say going veg is one of the top things you can do for the environment. So, I resolve, er, ripple to finally do it. Maybe then ripping, raw food vegan Bif Naked will go out with me.

Vague-a-bond 01-01 22:22
Queen Sabine, you are SOMETHING! Totally beautiful & an asset to the planet. I'm so glad to know you. Happiness and joy in the eclectic and ever surprising journey ahead.

earthgirl

sixteen_

So here it was, a brand, spanking new year. And with it a whole new perspective. An almost completely new and improved me! A new agenda. A new opportunity. To be and to make a difference. In my life. In my community. In my world. In the universe. In the omniverse.

Bye-bye to the timid Sabine Olivia Solomon tiptoeing around trying to get things done. Enduring the whiny critiques of my doubters and adversaries with a shrug and a sigh. The taunts and sniggers and back talk. Backing down when I should have been bucking up.

Whatever fate had in store, I was willing and able to face it head on and held high. Yep, somehow I'd actually become part of something bigger than my little idea of empowerment and conscious living. And while I knew it was due to my own initiative, my delicious now mended boyfriend had also made a profoundly profound contribution. In oh so many ways.

Item 1: His calm, determined, informed yet open personality.

Item 2: His circle of equally engaged and engaging comrades (even the mouthy obnoxious ones).

Item 3: His deep integrity and interest in the world...and in me and my deep integrity and interest in the world!

And finally Item 4: The most excellent and thoughtful gifties he presented to me in the form of two highly intellectual and stimulating books I'd have never known about before.

One was *Rules for Radicals*, a scruffy, doggy-eared paperback how-to-agitate guide written way back in 1971. Entire lifetimes ago. The other this ancient hardcover with the excellent title of *The Air-Conditioned Nightmare* by Henry Miller, some American writer in Paris in the thirties, famous for smutty books that were banned in the US.

This wasn't one of those. It was a different kind of naughty.

"That book's so crazy prescient," Vray said as I opened the paper bag and pulled out the weathered book and contemplated what he actually meant by prescient which wasn't a word in my current vocabulary but I presumed should be. "He wrote it during World War II when he visited the States cause his dad was dying and seriously, he could be talking about greed, selfishness, terrorism – all the stuff going on now."

"How did you know about this?" I asked.

"It was on the bookshelf downstairs and air-conditioning bugs the crap out of me," he said matter-of-factly. "Anyway check this, '*What do we have to offer the world beside the superabundant loot which we recklessly plunder from the earth under the maniacal idea that this insane idea actually represents progress and enlightenment?*' Or this, '*The automobile*

181 **earthgirl**

stands out in my mind as the very symbol of falsity and illusion.' It's unbelievable. He could see the future back then."

"Yeah," I nodded, but mostly I was thinking how incredible Vray was. And hoping I could be amazing enough to keep up with him and his ideas. And live up to my own new expectations of myself.

When I flipped through the book later, I noticed that Vray (or someone) had highlighted the more profound passages. But even though it was punchy and insightful, it was also kind of whiney. Smartypants Henry Miller was Mr. Grumpypants. He was obviously clever, but what did he ever do besides complain?

Where was the action to back up the reaction when he wrote, '*A new world is not made simply by trying to forget the old. A new world is made with a new spirit, with new values*'?

I guess that's where the other book came in. It was even more intriguing, despite the somewhat contradictory title of *Rules for Radicals*. If you were a true radical then didn't you say FU to rules and regulations?

Anyway, I was pretty flattered. I'd never considered myself exactly radical. Different, okay, but not in that extreme rebel way. Then again, the more I read, the more I realized that I was living totally outside the normal status-quo-suburban-box my family and former compadres lived in.

Every day proved this more and more. I was definitely not the least bit normal any more. And proud of it.

According to these "rules," the organizer should seek out controversy and attack apathy. And clearly without even realizing it I was the organizer since it was my genius idea to put together Be Green Day and the anti-postering postering blitz. Not to mention my brilliant new soon-to-be-hatched plans.

Sadly, my recruitment sucked. So far I'd only been able to recruit an army of one (do boyfriends even count as recruits?). Two, if you counted me. Hardly the force needed to change the world on a grand scale. But you've got to start somewhere.

e a r t h g i r l
[Jan. 8th | 09:49pm]
[mood | hopeful]
[music | bloody mother f#&%ing asshole – martha wainwright]

A NOT SHORT ENUF LIST OF OUTRAGES AND INJUSTICES:

1. TOO MUCH PACKAGING - Why does stuff come wrapped in 10x more plastic and paper than the actual thing? RESIST and INSIST ON LESS!

2. POP MACHINES IN SCHOOLS - Aren't some of your classmates chunky and unhealthy enough without sucking back more sugar each day? FIGHT THE POWER.

3. THE LACK OF ENVIRONMENTAL EDUCATION AND AWARENESS TAUGHT IN SCHOOLS. Demand more.

4. GIANORMOUS SUPPOSED SPORTS UTILITY VEHICLES – Cuz everyone knows you need a truck-car for the

treacherous paved city street to go play tennis or get supersoft toilet paper for your very special bum.

5. PEOPLE WHO DON'T RECYCLE. This should be a crime.

6. CELLPHONE MANIA. Enough already!

7. SELFISHNESS AND RUDENESS. Nuff said.

link   read 7 | post

altalake 01-08 21:58
I eagerly anticipate the update on your exploits of exploitation.

Vague-a-bond 01-08 22:22
8 - People who wear stinky choke and gag inducing perfume and chemically yucky fragrance in movie theaters, on planes or to yoga class! Cough, cough, gag, gag.

Stryker1992 01-08 23:23
Who the hell are U people? And why don't U shut THE FUCK up!?!!

Nostradamnus 93 1-9-10:10
You and your eco-pussy friends are a bunch of reactionary whiners.

Global warming is a CROCK. Remember, there was once something called an ice age brainiacs. The planet gets cold, the planet gets warm.

As for pollution — its a MYTH. Its simply the redistru-
bution of materials that already existed on this planet.
Unless you know something about alien imports, you
people and your green bullshit are dead wrong. Chillaxe
fools.

Initially I was jarred by Stryker's meanie posts. And
Nostradamnus's wacko prophecies with their almost logical
idiocy. Plus I couldn't help wondering if their messages
came courtesy of Darren Mankowsky or Corey Crawford
(or even, yikes, Carmen in an x-treme-bitch mood?). I
wanted to counterpost something so clever and seething it
tore the pathetic comments to shreds.

Then I realized that would just lower me to their level. A
place I refused to even visit ever again.

I suppose everyone is entitled to his or her opinion, however misguided. And so far my brilliant blog had definitely
attracted more supporters than detractors. There were
bound to be a few cowardly bullies ready to lunge.

It was naive to think that this new way of living would
be easy peasy. That converting closed-minded dum-dums
would be a snap. Nothing that mattered ever was.

Curiously, school wasn't as horrendous as before the
break. Amped by the validation of Vray, Ruby and the gang
of thinky, talky amazing people, I felt completely empowered. And not afraid to voice my resistance to things and situations I considered unjust or out-of-whack. Someone had
to stand up and right the wrongs and that someone was
definitely going to be me.

When I said we should lobby the school board to add classes on environmentalism, Mrs. Rubin did her best poker face and pretended she was interested. She even gave me a list of school board administrators so I could write letters.

"I'm not saying it's a bad idea, Sabine," she said with her precision principal voice. "It's just that curriculum changes are a long and arduous process. By the time anything happens, you won't even be a student here."

"I'm not doing this for myself. It's for the students after me."

"That's a wonderful position, but your immediate focus should be your grades and getting accepted into university."

But I had plans and I was going to carry them out. Being a defender of the planet was too important to let a bit of resistance sway me.

And so what if Darren Mankowsky and his lunkhead teammates destroyed my petition to abolish pop and snack machines in the school caf.

"Their sponsorship pays for our teams, idiot," Darren roared as he pulverized the collection of two dozen signatures I'd convinced out of Alexis Shaw's posse.

"The companies behind those machines engage in questionable labor practices, force unhealthy products on growing bodies, not to mention limit the choice in the global playing field," I explained.

"Oh, shut the fuck up already. All you and your stupid ranting will do is make our money disappear!"

"There are ways to pay for school sports without selling out to corporate shills," I said calmly as I gathered up the fragments of the petition. "It's called fundraising."

"You're an idiot, Sabine."

"Takes one to know one," I said, unintentionally lowering myself to his very limited communication level. "I hear chocolate-covered almonds are popular."

"That's so funny, I forgot to laugh. And for your information, Carmen thinks you and your eco-crap is idiotic, too." Then he and his no-neck gang tromped off, laughing.

So there I was considering a more stealth campaign to encourage healthier eating when I felt some faintly familiar fingers tap my shoulder.

Ella silently jerked her head toward the bathroom as she practically dragged me after her. She looked very nervous.

"He's a first-class ass," she said as she fired up a disgusting cigarette. "So how are you?"

"Fine." I was starting to wonder if these random intrusions proved everyone around me had gone squirrelly.

Ella nodded and bobbed her head as smoke flared from her nostrils. Then suddenly she reached into this massive leather purse I'd never seen before and pulled out a small sparkly package.

"What's this?" I asked as she thrust it toward me.

"Fancy pants. For your first-class ass."

"I didn't get you anything." It felt weird taking it.

"That's okay," she shrugged. "Open it already!"

I untangled the ribbon from the tissue paper and tore into the little purple packet. Inside was a pair of leopard-spotted thongs with pink lace trim.

They were absolutely hideous.

"I was going to get you those abstinence panties," she

huffed between puffs. "The ones that say things like, 'I'm waiting for marriage.' But then I saw these and you have to buy the others on the net and like who're we kidding and what if we never get married?"

"Thanks," I said, because it was the only thing to say. It's not like I was going to discuss my personal life with her despite this sudden burst of kindness.

I bunched them in a ball and stuffed them into the side pocket of my pack. I had no idea what to do with them, since modeling them for Vray didn't exactly make the list. Tossing them would be wasteful, so I'd do the next best thing and give them to Clare.

"It was weird over the holidays," Ella nodded, chugging frantically on the cigarette. "Not emailing you from Ixtapa or stopping by when I got back from the airport like I always do."

"You could've emailed," I said, even though I don't know how I'd have felt if she had.

Anyway, I was so busy with Vray and work and all the new and, I had to admit, more open and interesting people in my world to miss alerts about her dad's funky stomach or how she sneaked out and drank tequila shots with some college guys on the beach. Not to be snarky, but that's how I felt.

And why shouldn't I? She'd abandoned me so I'd done the only rational thing under the circumstances. I moved on.

"Anyway, just so you know, I think your ideas to improve the school are really good," she said, tossing her butt into the toilet and flushing with her foot in one swift, practiced movement. "Especially the food reform, no matter what Darren and his fukwits say."

"Thanks," I said, completely shocked that not only had Ella cornered me on her own, but she seemed to have formed an opinion, too.

"Carmen was a bit harsh," she went on. "I told her but she kept insisting we needed to teach you a lesson cause you were being such a pill, which you were, but in the end I guess the joke was on us cause you ditched us right back, huh?"

I didn't know what to say. This stunning self-awareness from Ella was unprecedented in the many years I'd known her. On the one hand I wanted to encourage it, but on the other didn't want to hurt her feelings and confirm that what she'd said was true. So I did the only sane thing in the circumstances. Got out of there pronto.

"I've gotta get to English," I said, pulling open the door. "But thanks for the talk and the fancy pants."

e a r t h g i r l
[Jan. 11th | 08:33pm]
[mood | proactive]
[music | sunshowers – MIA]

In the interests of my willingly captive (and captivating!) audience, some thoughts on the Rules for Radicals and their effectiveness.

Rule #3. *Go outside the experience of your opponent.* This

will create fear, confusion and retreat. Still waiting for the retreat part, but 2 outta 3 ain't bad!

Rule #6. A good tactic is fun. It's important that your people are having fun. If I count my people as me, then yes, I am having fun. So far anyway! :)

Rule #9. The threat is more terrifying than the action. Talk about understatements, my campaign to ban vending machines has made me the school leper. And though it sounds gross and sad, it's also sort of thrilling.

Oddly, being radical doesn't feel all that radical. It kind of seems like being honest and full of integrity.

link   read 6 | post
www.vcn.bc.ca/citizens-handbook/rules.html

altalake 01-11 23:58
I recommend subvertising, the modern art of ad and billboard defacement. A great means of expression + getting your yayas out.
www.billboardliberation.com
www.cacophony.org

lacklusterlulu 01.12 00:57
Been there, done that and totally agree! Except for the getting caught and in trouble for vandalism part, it was seriously kewl. Radicalz Rule!

seventeen_

It took about two weeks of research and location scouting before I finally hatched my biggish radical action – an anti-SUV campaign, which in my head I called Project U-SUX. But never on paper or online since I didn't want to leave a trail or do anything that might incriminate me in any way, especially with the parentals. Wouldn't want to alert them to my new subversive activities or I'd risk being put under house arrest for like forever, or at least until I was twenty-one.

So despite my nonstop head butting at school, I was heads down at home to keep them off the scent. And my sweet compliant doppelganger personality had been working like a charm. That and because the units were supremely busy. Dad with his annual squash tournament and Mom with the debut of yet another home decorating and useless stuff store.

Needless to say, if there were an award for cool-as-a-cucumber daughter-of-the-year, I was the hands-down winner. Oh, how little they knew the new me.

But to do it right, to really pull off the U-SUX plan, I needed help. And that's where Vray would come in. To be my accomplice, not only in love but also in the battle against forces destroying the community and the planet (and almost him!). This would not only deepen our shared commitment to the cause, but to each other.

"So, um, this a sex thing?" Vray asked hopefully as I led him across the backyard toward the big oak and the remains of my old treehouse.

I shook my head. There was about six inches of old snow hardened to crusty after days of melt-freeze. We shuffled across the slippery white surface, suspended momentarily before our boots crunched loudly through to the ground. *Shhhhh-twink-unk!* I loved that sound and that feeling. It was like controlled falling.

"You never know," Vray said as I dropped his hand and started climbing the ladder nailed to the tree trunk. "Unconsciously it might be what you had in mind, though you could've brought a blanket."

"It's not," I said seriously as he practically climbed over me to get up the tree. The weight of him against my legs and bum was distracting, but I refused to be distracted.

This wasn't a game. I was on an important mission.

"So, what's with the secret hideout?" he asked, pushing himself up into what I called the Moon Room when I was little. He mostly used his good arm since even though his collarbone was way better, it still wasn't one hundred percent.

"Just a special place and I have to tell you something special, away from nosy sisters and parents and just, people."

"All right," he said, plopping down and shushing himself back against the wall. "Give 'er."

"Well, when we first met, you told me how they were going to drill for oil in Alaska and confuse and kill all the caribou. Then all this weird weather keeps happening everywhere and that voodoo flu epidemic crosses the ocean and then out of nowhere you get taken out by an SUV," I said, breathlessly realizing there was so much to explain.

"Heap of shitty coincidences for sure."

"You don't believe in coincidences. Everything happens for reasons, always," I insisted.

"Yeah, jerks don't know how to drive."

"No, everything happens according to some bigger epic plan, fate and destiny and karmic reasons. I get pelted with garbage on my bike, you get nailed by an S.U.X. It has to mean something and there have to be consequences and the amazing thing is we can create consequences."

Vray was leaning forward now, looking at me very intensely.

"And?" he asked with a tone that suggested he was pretty amped about everything I was saying. Exactly the way I knew he would be.

"This," I said, pulling my one, and so far only, hand-blocked, magic-markered U-SUX poster out of my pocket and unfolding it.

"I don't get it," he said.

"I've done some research. Reconnaissance or spying even, mostly on these midtown GM dealerships. I picked them cause GM and Chev make so many SUVs and also Hummers plus they own Cadillac who make those stupid Navigators and Escalade things. And I found this place and it's amazing. No videocameras on the far lot, so I thought we could go really late at night and put these on the cars."

"What, like under the windshield wipers?"

"No, that won't do anything. I want to paste them over windows and make a real mess," I said, my arms flying around now to show the magnitude of the venture. "But the glue has to be serious, not something they can just blast away with a powerwasher, so I asked the guy at Thompson's Hardware and he says this epoxy mix is so crazy sticky that if you get it on your fingers it rips the flesh right off so we'll need to wear medical gloves, but I'm all over that, too. Already scoffed a box from my dad's stash in the basement."

Vray stared at me for a long time, paying very close attention to every detail.

"So? What do you think?" I was almost bursting with excitement.

"It's completely lame, no offense."

"It's not lame. It's proactive and radical!"

"What, like your pop-machine ban? And some tree-hugging class? People are on the frontlines of this battle risking jail time by breaking into medical labs to free animals or staring down chainsaws to protest logging practices. C'mon, gluing posters on windshields? It's total amateur hour."

I couldn't believe what I was hearing! My open-minded, incredibly progressive and lovely boyfriend was being such a...asshole! It was like someone had snatched the real Vray and replaced him with some deviant, snippy replicant.

Besides, who was he to talk? Aside from playing in some crappy band at a protest gig here and there, I didn't see him

rescuing crash test bunnies or saving any trees. As if he was
some big front-line cutting-edge radical!

"I bring you to my special place, tell you my secret plans
and you're slamming me?" I said, surprised by my own
anger. I couldn't believe it. We were having our first ever
fight.

"You should've brought me here for sex," he half
laughed.

"You can leave anytime you like," I snapped.

"That's probably a good idea," he said, pulling on his hat
and sliding his bum toward the entrance. "Best you've had
today, actually."

"That was just plain mean," I yelled as he backed down
the ladder.

"I'll call you later," he called back across the yard, over
the *crunch-crunch* of his boots. "After you calm down and
realize I'm right."

"I'm perfectly calm," I shouted back at him.

The jerk.

e a r t h g i r l
[Jan. 20th | 5:16pm]
[mood | #@&+!^*]
[music | Rockstar Boyfriend – Tuuli]

Rule #5. Ridicule is a very potent weapon in the radical
arsenal. It infuriates and embarrasses the opposition.

This is apparently extremely true. Astonishingly actually.
However, it's important to remember, the *organizer* is not

the *opposition.* Shocking though it is, sometimes radicals get a bit confused that they're all on the same side. Maybe it's the pressure of being on the leading edge.

So remember fellow radicals, united we stand, divided we are royally screwed. And get bruised feelings.

link   read 3 | post

Vague-a-bond 01-20 19:02
What's up bean? You don't read like the usual bubbly you. Hope there's no trouble in your paradise of *truth* and love. Big Hugs, Ms. C.

e a r t h g i r l
[January 20th | 07:09pm]
Whoa, Cassie! Are you a witch (Glinda-good-witch) or psychic superpower mind reader or something? Little blip confirmed, but nothing that won't resolve shortly. Me thinks. Me hopes anyway!

To say Vray's response to my genius idea was not the reaction I expected would be the understatement of my life. Even though I was absolutely furious, I found myself crying uncontrollably when I took a bubblebath to calm my jangled nerves. My hot tears dripped onto the mountains of suds, melting holes to the tepid bathwater.

I felt so defeated and so frustrated I felt defeated.

After my soak and sulk, I calmed down. I realized my idea was undercooked and yes, okay, maybe babyish. A germ instead of a virus. Paper and glue? This wasn't an arts and crafts project. It was a powerful, radical statement. More like spraypaint and smashed windows (without actually smashing windows). And maybe Vray's reaction was just his way of pushing me without being pushy.

I mean clearly he had been involved in some defiant things before he met me. How else to explain the superhero confabs with Finn and Eric. From hearing them play it obviously wasn't for the band to practice. Maybe it was all so extreme and subversive, he didn't tell me or include me because he loved me too much to put me at risk.

Still, he didn't have to laugh at Project U-SUX. But rather than wallow, I decided to study for tomorrow's math test. So I hunkered down at my desk and tried to concentrate and pretend everything was normal. That trigonometry was the balm for my bruised heart.

"Hey there," Mom said with that annoying cheery mom voice as she suddenly appeared in my space despite the partially closed door. "What's going on?

"Math test," I mumbled.

"Then you could probably use more light," she said helpfully as she unhelpfully turned on the light, making me flinch from its brightness.

"Not a good time," I said, hoping she'd retreat before she saw my puffy red eyes.

"Never is with you," she sighed as she sat down on my bed.

How is it parents had that uncanny knack for appearing and annoying you at the most inopportune moments?

Was it genetic? Radar? Some kind of weird embedded chip?

"Honey, I need to talk to you. I mean, we need to talk," Mom said.

This was definitely going to be a doozy so I didn't even bother to look up from my book. As if that would stop her. Ha!

"I don't want you to feel like I'm barging in on you or ambushing you, but we never seem to talk any more," she said, clearly aware that she was doing both those things, but not seeming to care. "I'd have called or texted but your cell is always off, which isn't a bad thing though it's a bit odd."

"First you complain I use it too much. Now you complain I don't use it enough?" I was so not in the mood for this right now. Agh!

"You're right. It's just you've just been so remote lately. You do know we can talk about anything." Mom emphasized the word *anything* and for a fleeting moment I wondered if she'd been going to parenting-your-teen talks.

"Okay," I answered, suspecting this could definitely be the dreaded sex talk we'd mercifully managed to avoid all these years. "I get it and no, I'm not on drugs and yes, I'm totally fine, thank you."

"We know that. It's just I couldn't help but notice how close you and Vray have gotten recently," she continued, trying to sound like my pal. "And we've respected that and given you space and trusted you to have good instincts and make good choices."

I nodded and bit my tongue and tried to pretend her

concern was cute and endearing and not as annoying and intrusive as it actually was. Especially at this particular moment in my life, given that my relationship (if there still was one) was now hanging by a thread.

I could feel my tummy tighten.

"I'm not going to ask if you've done it or even what you've done because I really don't want to know," she insisted, talking quickly enough for me to notice she was probably almost as uncomfortable as she was making me. "That's private between you and Vray."

"Good," I sighed, as I put my face in the book I was not reading.

"It's just I remember what it was like to be young and think everything was so urgent and important," she stormed on like a tornado in a trailer park.

"Vray is important," I said, immediately regretting that I was buying into her baiting. And suddenly feeling like I wasn't going to hold it together. Plus I'd forgotten how effective the silent treatment was in situations like these. Dum-dum me.

"I know," she said. "And I've told you we think he's lovely and good to you."

"Glad you approve," I snorted, even though I could care less if they did or not. Like they even understood me at all. Like they even had the first clue.

"I just hope you're being responsible about birth control and sexually transmitted diseases, not to mention your emotional needs," Mom said with the formality of a well-practiced speech, even though she was trying to act all casual.

"Your emotional well being is as important as the other stuff, you know. More important, maybe."

Yeah, tell me about it, I thought, doing my best to keep myself from crumbling into a sobbing mess while willing her out of the room.

"Aw, Mom, do we have to talk about this?" I groaned instead. At this very moment when I may have just had my heart crushed and stomped on by this boyfriend you're telling me is so lovely and amazing.

"Yes," she nodded a bit nervously.

"No, we don't," I said emphatically.

"Okay, then," she said, sounding as relieved as I was. "But if you want to talk, about anything at all, you know where I am."

Yeah, yeah, I thought, nodding and waving her away. Just don't expect me to come looking for you any time soon.

eighteen_

It had been almost twenty-four hours and I still hadn't heard from Vray. Nada, by phone, email, text or carrier pigeon. I was shocked and heartsick. And I felt silly and ashamed of how far I'd fallen. Suspended on the surface only to crash to the hard, frozen ground beneath.

I wasn't sure what to do besides pretend everything was normal and cross my fingers and toes it actually would be again. I suppose I could have just caved and called him, but that would make me like every other stupid girl who groveled her way back into the cuddleship. Plus I wasn't the one in the wrong.

I wasn't the one making fun of him and his plans. His ideas. His integrity and commitment.

After school I took the bus to the co-op for my shift, happy to be busy and not waiting by the phone. But when I walked past the notice board where Vray and I had first met and mind-melded, it felt like a punch in the gut.

Something I had to recover from pretty quickly when Tom spotted me.

"Sabine, Natalka went home with the flu so there's a dozen boxes for the body aisles. Sorry to swamp you, but it's gotta get done," he said as I marched solemnly toward the stockroom to ditch my coat and backpack. "Hey, you okay? You look a bit pasty yourself."

"I'm fine," I nodded. I mean, technically from a physical health standpoint, I was. From a mental health perspective, not so much. Plus I doubted a slight dose of lovesickness counted as a real illness.

"Take it easy and do what you can," he said. "Can't afford to have everyone around here knocked out."

Tom was a nice guy and a good boss. Concerned and conscientious without being bossy or nosy. He trusted you to do what he asked without much fuss. I bet he was a great dad to his little twin boys.

For a nanosecond I considered asking him what to do about Vray before realizing how immature and silly, not to mention inappropriate, it would sound asking my boss for boyfriend advice.

So it was me and the teatree shampoo and verbena conditioner for the night. And some weird tribal music CD I might enjoy at any other point in my life. I wished Ruby was around but she'd gone to Costa Rica with Hayley on a last-minute deal. That was both a good and bad thing. Bad because I couldn't solicit her advice. Good because I wouldn't be dragging her into my drama, which was probably only dramatic to me anyway.

Surprisingly, the shelf stocking was very soothing. Meditative, even. Before I'd even realized, Tom lowered the front lights, a sign the store would soon be closing. Four hours had disappeared in a blink.

I finished up the row I was working on, closed the last half-empty (half-full?) carton of body lotions and carried it to the stockroom.

"Your boyfriend's here," Tom said, leaning into the back where I was pulling on my jacket.

For a second I didn't know what he was talking about, but then Vray poked his curly head through the storeroom door.

"Car's out front, I'll meet you there," he said normally. Like I'd seen him five minutes ago and everything was absolutely fine. Or like I'd just woken up from a coma or a bout of amnesia or something. "Thought you'd like a ride home," he smiled, heading back out, the door swinging in his wake.

Vray was in his mom's silver hybrid, pulled up to the curb in the No Stopping zone. He reached across the seat to get the passenger door from the inside, reminding me how polite and thoughtful he could be.

When he wanted to be. The hypocrite.

"Your mom said you were working," he practically chirped. "Figured I'd surprise you."

"I thought you never drive in a car alone," I said, wondering if I should have walked past him to catch the bus. If getting in was giving in, or simply my desire to hear him out like the civilized person I was.

"I'm not alone," he beamed, leaning over to kiss my cheek. I pulled away, practically bumping my head on the window.

I glared at him.

"What?" he asked, huffing into his cupped hand. "Bad breath?"

"Bad manners," I snorted.

"Am I missing something?" he asked as he pulled out and started driving.

"I'm sorry," I answered flatly.

"For what?" He seemed genuinely mystified, which left me more than a bit mystified.

"Didn't we have a fight?" I asked, now wondering if I had imagined the whole thing.

"Why? Because you told me some big secret plot and I pointed out it was half-baked?"

"Well, it's evolved since then."

"Oh yeah, to what?"

"Spraypaint," I announced, surprising myself with the big announcement. Not to mention how quickly all was forgiven.

"Nice," he nodded as he signaled and pulled into a church parking lot. "Not quite what the guys and I had in mind, but closer."

"You told them?" I was floored. "That was private. What else did you tell them about us?"

"Relax," he said softly as he ran his hand up my arm. "I said you had an idea and we started jamming and came up with a way to seriously pull it off."

I just stared at his hand, which was now wrapped around my wrist like a bracelet. My breath came loudly out of my nose as I yanked my arm back.

"You're unbelievable. First you make fun of my idea.

Then instead of apologizing for being rude and snippy, you betray me to your friends."

"Okay, okay, sorry. But come on, Sabine, you wanted to put stickers on cars like a little girl," he said calmly. "So last night me and the boys looked at the lot you mentioned. And you're right. No cameras, not to mention some sketch lighting out back. So we started thinking, why go for kiddie shit when we could really fuck 'em over by torching a few cars." His eyes were practically twinkling in the dark as he talked. "Same effort really, but much bigger effect."

"Ha, ha, very funny."

"The E-L-F took down a Hummer dealership in California and got away with it. No reason we couldn't do the same thing here."

"Those cars, that dealership, that's someone's business," I said, matching his even tone.

"Yeah, and spraypainting is vandalizing someone's business," he replied, equally calm.

"It's not blowing things up. I think that's called terrorism."

"Not if we're the good guys. Besides, you're the one who keeps saying someone has to protect and defend the earth."

"Stop acting like it's logical! It's completely insane. And why are you acting like it was my idea? This was not remotely what I had in mind and you know it."

"I think it's exactly what you had in mind. You were just afraid to go there so soon."

"Oh sure, hijack my idea and twist it into something crazy destructive, not to mention totally illegal and dangerous and I started it?"

"It's not against the law if it's against society and the laws of nature," he said calmly. "There's something much bigger at work here. I know you see it. Admit it, if not to me at least to yourself."

I sat staring straight ahead. I was afraid to look at him. Afraid of what else he might say and what I might say back. Afraid he would twist my words again and throw them back in my face. Afraid of what he was capable of doing.

And of what I might discover I was capable of, too.

"Please take me home," I said quietly.

Vray started the car and we drove to my house in silence.

"I know it's big," he said in a soothing voice as he pulled into the driveway. "Sleep on it. You'll see, you'll feel different tomorrow."

He leaned toward me to kiss me goodnight. I wanted so, so badly to move away, but the way he hovered drew me in. Hypnotized me. Instead I tried not to kiss back, but it was like my lips had a mind of their own.

I hoped my mind didn't have a mind of its own.

"Just promise me you'll at least think about it," Vray said gently.

I took a deep breath and nodded as I snapped the car door open, slid out and slammed it behind me. He waved, like everything was completely normal as he peeled away into the night. The car fishtailed on the slush and snow-covered street, leaving behind squiggly black marks.

Big. Shocking. Confusing. Exciting. Terrifying. I could keep listing things, but mostly the list was a way to fill the space between us as it grew larger and larger.

• • •

I didn't sleep on it. Not that I didn't try. I tossed and turned and flipped and flopped like a rowboat on a stormy ocean.

And in the morning, I did feel different. Completely exhausted and so anxious I thought I might puke. But I felt different in other ways, too. In more surprising and even frightening ways, I understood what he wanted and why (though he really should have asked me before blabbing to his buddies). And even though what he was proposing was completely outrageous and verging on totally insane, in some small ways I could also see his point.

I could see the truth of it. The intention behind the insanity. And maybe he was right, and all he'd really done was take my idea to the next level. Take it somewhere relevant and significant. Take it to the place where any clear-thinking, truly radical mind would go. A place my own intentions and actions were struggling to get to.

Yes, it was mega. It was reactionary. It was dangerous. It was criminal. It was wrong. It was all those things and so much more.

It was also too complicated to just dismiss outright. Even if it was an act of destruction, it was also in a backward way an act of creation. If they (or we?) pulled it off, it would create something, too.

Controversy. Outrage. Discussion. Change. And wasn't all that what I wanted the earthgirl to stand for? Maybe this was the logical culmination of my own re-evolution from my growing anti-consumer insights, to gravitating toward things like the Suzuki Foundation and Ruckus Society. From encouraging my friends and schoolmates into behaving more responsibly, to my own small gestures of civil disgust and disobedience.

Maybe, even though it was obviously absolutely the wrong thing to do, it was also the right thing. The very thing that should be done.

e a r t h g i r l
[January 22nd | 1:03am]
[mood | pooped]
[music | i hear noises – tegan + sara]

Some questions to ponder on the rocky radical road to re-evolutionary thought...

When is being different really just being the same? How far is too far? Is it ever okay to break the law? Is fear a good motivation? Is love a better one? What does it take? How far will you take it?

If not you, WHO?

If not now, WHEN?

THE END JUSTIFIES THE MEANS. But does it? Does it really?

link   read 5 | post
www.wikipedia.org/wiki/Activism

altalake 01-23 03:36
Oooooooo, existential crisis alert. Sorry, I'm
staying away from this one, already got four of
my own!

onederful 01-23 06:39
Don't know if the end justifies the means
but justification is the means to justify
almost everything in the end.

Vague-a-bond 01-24 10:04
BIG questions and chaos. Just remember chaos is growth. And
growth is change. And yes, change is scary, but it's also necessary and inevitable. Without growth there is stagnation. So
embrace the chaos. Hug it close.

I wasn't exactly feeling like myself. Who I was feeling like
was altogether another mystery.

If I were a smoker, I'd be smoking. Chugging on butts
the way Ella did and my life depended on it. If I were a nail-
biter, I'd have gnawed my fingertips bloody. If I were a cut-
ter, I'd be scratching and twitching. If I were a binger, I'd be
purging. Yeah, if I were more like so many of my majorly
messed-up schoolmates, I'd be screwing things up to the
very best of my rather significant abilities.

Except I wasn't any of those things. I wasn't over the
edge, even though it seemed like I might fall off it. Even if
I was standing on the brink, staring into this new infinite
abyss of possibility that was both terrifyingly awesome and
awesomely terrifying. I just wanted to be sure my decision

was mine. Not motivated by love or loyalty or hormones or peer pressure or stupidity.

It was lunchtime, but I had no appetite. So I walked out into the brisk, gray January day and let the shock of the cold burn my throat and nostrils.

There weren't many people outside, but under the stoner tree I saw Shane McCardle.

Good old weatherproof Shane.

He was bundled up in his Guatemalan jacket, which he'd winterized with a puffy vest. On his head he wore a sheepskin aviator hat and his glittens had the fingers cut out (no doubt for fast access). I wandered toward him silently pointing at his pack on the bench beside him. He moved it out of the way and patted the seat.

"Ah, the bold and controversial Ms. Solomon. To what do I owe this honor?"

"Can I ask you something, confidentially?"

"Absolutely. I owe you. All the annoying stuff you've been up to has really taken the heat off me."

"What would you do if someone you cared about wanted you to do something illegal?"

"Ah, Sabine, if you wanted some smoke, you just had to ask," Shane smiled, pulling a baggy of spongy green weed from his pocket.

"It's more illegal than that," I said, watching his fingers, which though extremely long were also amazingly nimble as he expertly and efficiently whipped up a rollie before my eyes.

"More illegal?" he said, raising his eyebrow. "Some people would say breaking the law is breaking the law, end of story."

"Says the guy breaking the law," I answered too quickly, realizing if I insulted him he probably wouldn't be terribly helpful.

"We talking about that oooh edgy boyfriend of yours?" he asked, giving me the sideways eyeball.

"How do you even know about him?"

"I know things," he answered tapping his temple.

"It's not him. It's one of his idiot friends," I said. "That's why I can't talk to him about it. He's not exactly objective." Whew, that sounded even feasible for thinking on the fly.

Shane nodded like he understood and believed me. "F-Y-I, this is me protesting outdated laws. Draconian, repressive, regressive legislation."

"By supporting biker gangs and criminals?"

"I grow my own. I'm an eco-preneur." He passed me the spliffy and for a second I was tempted. "I call this one Tumbleweed. Go easy or you might fall down."

I nodded him off.

"Nature's gift," he sighed, popping it into his mouth and flicking a lighter to life. "Okay, will this thing hurt anybody, besides if this person or people get nailed for it?"

"Hopefully not physically, but definitely financially," I said carefully. "I mean, if it's pulled off okay."

"Hmmm," he mused as he hauled on the joint. "Well, if it were me deciding to play, and I think that's really what you're asking, basically I'd ask if I was going along for a cheap thrill or cause I was into it, too."

"I'm not talking about me," I insisted, even though I was asking a guy well acquainted with the edge if I should step over it.

"Whatever," Shane said, leaning his head back against the tree. "You're a smart girl. I think you already know what you're gonna do."

And as he said it, I realized he might actually be right.

e a r t h g i r l
[January 27th | 10:03pm]
[mood | contemplative]
[music | | Summon You - S/P/O/O/N]

The Daily Thought Bubble: TERRA-ism vs. Terrorism. Terrorism vs. TERRA-ism.

Is defending the planet from destruction the same thing as attacking and destroying innocent people and targets? The FBI, CIA and CSIS say al-Qaeda and the ELF are the same.

But how is killing innocent people riding the subway or on holiday or going to work the same as "inflicting economic damage to business and industry that threaten the planet"?

That threaten our home? Our mother? Our very existence?

link   read 6 | post
www.oeom.org

lacklusterlulu 01-27 11:57
So NOT the same! Apples and shoelaces. Ideology is personal and you can't say one is even like the other. Unless you're some fascist, self-centered Ayn Rand-ian.

Stryker1988 01-28 00:23
**FuckOffLeftWingFuckFaceCommies!!! If U hate freedom and capitil-
ism so much then leave and go to some communist dictater republic
of hell! The only reason U can even bitch is cuz yer priviledged losers with to much time on yer hands! GOFUCKYERSELFS!
www.lomborg.com/**

Vague-a-bond 01-28 00:43
Sensing some minor hostility and difference of opinions from
our new friend Stryker. Careful, stress causes heart disease
and other ailments. Try some yoga, meditation or visualiza-
tion. Namaste.

Stryker1988 01-28 01:06
VISUALIZE MYFOOT KICKING YER FAT ASS!

earthbound01 01-28
Why don't you block this scary neanderthal from posting here?

onederful 01-29 16:23 (link) Select
Freedom of speech also includes the freedom
to be an idiot.

e a r t h g i r l
[January 28th | 03:51pm]
And who knows, maybe some of our ideas and actions will
influence his.

nineteen_

"Told you she'd go for it," Vray boasted to Finn and Eric as we gathered in his room for the first "official" confab. His mom was lecturing at yet another conference in California and his dad was working late at the university, again.

"Do you even have parents?" I asked him once. "Or did you just make them up like your name?"

"Raised by wolves," he growled.

As for his supposed brainiac brother, I'd yet to meet him either, since he was always at a lab or the library studying. If I hadn't seen actual family photos, I might have thought Vray lived in this big gorgeous house all by his lonesome. Or with his perma-guest pals.

Eric the conspiracy theorist glared at me sideways like he was still doubtful about my decision. I didn't blame him. I'd probably be suspicious of me, too. Heck, I was me and I was suspicious of me.

"It was my idea," I reminded him.

"Hardly," Eric scoffed. "You were just carrying a germ which you happened to cough onto a higher organism. Us!"

"Nice visual," Finn laughed as he stumbled around the

room fake coughing and wiping his hands on the chair, Vray's head, duvet and stacks of books.

"No, good metaphor," Vray said. "Sabine's like Patient Zero for the virus and she passed it onto us and it mutated into a new super virus."

"Too powerful for conventional forces to destroy," Eric agreed. "Even stockpiled vaccines can't stop us cause there are too many of us out there, mutating and ready for action."

"But not yet. I think we should do it around Earth Day," I said. "Contrast all the happy cuddly organized stuff."

"End of April's too far off," Vray said. "Too risky to wait."

"Not to mention a cheesy, faggy cliché," Eric added.

Man, was this guy ever not sarcastic and snarky?

"We definitely shouldn't sit on this too long," Finn said thoughtfully. "Too much chance for intervention or fucking up."

I nodded, as if what they were saying made complete sense. As if they were talking about booking another gig for their band or finding a summer job on a tree-planting crew. Except they weren't. We weren't.

"I took a look at the advance forecast," Vray said, pulling a piece of paper off his desk. "There's a warm front coming in next week and it's good to wait till the snow melts. Otherwise there's too much reflection and light."

"The full moon was two days ago, so it will be darker out, too," I said.

"Good thinking," Finn nodded. "Also less snow, less footprints."

"And a weeknight. Tuesday or Wednesday really late," Eric added. "Weekends leave too much chance of people passing by, getting suspicious."

"I don't know if I can get out on a school night," I said. "I mean, in the middle of the night?"

"Well, if you can't manage something as simple as that, maybe you'd better not bother," Eric snapped.

Even though I knew Eric was a smug idiot, the comment still made me feel incredibly stupid. And young. And useless. Maybe their parents didn't have a clue where they were half the time, but mine still occasionally monitored my comings and goings.

"Don't worry," Vray said softly. "We'll park down the street so they don't see or hear the car. You'll be back in bed before they even notice you've been gone."

"Definitely the cars on the back lot," Finn said. "No point breaking into the showroom. The video and alarm risk is too high. Besides, the SUVs inside have empty tanks and no batteries, they won't go up anyway."

"Exactly," Eric agreed. "The cars outside will have gas traces in their tanks and it's that vapor we need to catch."

"How do you even know that?" I asked, impressed and terrified by everything they knew and I hadn't even thought about.

"Chemistry," Eric said as if I was stupid. "Don't you know anything about chemistry?"

"Gloves at all times, balaclavas and black clothes. Socks,

too," Vray said. "Stuff you don't care about because we're going to torch it later. Shoes, too. Can't risk bringing home any whiffs of gas."

"I'll funnel fuel out of cars on the street," Eric said. "I'm probably being paranoid, but we can't risk getting traced back to some gas station surveillance system."

"Maybe we've got this all wrong," I blurted, as my body filled with anxiety.

"No, we're all over the details, Sabine," Finn said calmly. "It's all good."

"It's dangerous, but mostly it defeats the purpose of everything we're trying to achieve. To change," I said. Someone had to at least suggest this was outrageous and it obviously wasn't going to be one of them. "The only message we end up sending is that we know how to destroy things. Doesn't that make us as bad as they are? As bad as all the corporations and politician people destroying the planet?"

"You don't know fuck, Sabine," Eric sighed. "And you're not here to lecture us about things you know nothing about. I told Vray to keep you out of this, that you'd try to fuck us over."

"That's not what I'm doing," I insisted. I'm trying to stop it, I thought, but didn't bother saying since it was obvious and obviously not working.

"You're getting wound up for nothing, babe," Vray assured me. "We know what we're doing and we know it'll work."

"And I know all that will happen is an insurance compa-

earthgirl

ny will swoop in and replace all the stupid SUVs we trash. And that's if we don't get caught, hurt anyone or get killed!"

"Me and you both know you can find just as many reasons to talk yourself into it as talk yourself out," Vray said logically.

"I was a bit spooked at first, too," Finn confessed with a smile, like having solidarity in the shitting-my-pants department would help. "Nervous is good. We have to stay on our toes."

I looked from Vray to Finn to Eric and back to Vray again. They were obviously unmoved by my comments. Whether I was in or out, I was still complicit. I had started this avalanche and listening to them, to their certainty and conviction, I wasn't sure if I had the power I needed to stop it.

"We're doing it," Vray said defiantly. "We've been doing things for ages and it's time to graduate to the next level."

"What things?" I wanted to know and at the same time, not know. Not that I could possibly be in any deeper.

"Don't tell her shit," Eric hissed. "If she can't commit, she sure as shit doesn't need to know anything else."

I looked back at Vray, who shrugged.

"Look, if you're too scared, bail now," he said softly. "But this is happening. With or without you."

"It's a snowball coming down the mountain, Sabine," Finn agreed. "If you're not riding it, you better run like fuck."

I wanted to run, but it was icy and slippery and steep. So instead I just froze.

"How can we be sure we won't hurt anyone?" I asked, realizing some of the things that were obvious concerns of mine hadn't even seemed to cross their minds.

"Because we're not stupid," Eric sighed. "If you were paying attention, little girl, you might notice we're meticulous about every detail."

"Yeah, we're about inflicting economic damage," Finn said. "The E-L-F has done over forty million bucks' worth in over six hundred attacks without ever hurting anyone."

"What about that woman back in the eighties, the one with the Squamish Five gang? They injured ten people when they bombed the Litton plant in Scarborough. And they even phoned in a warning," I said, hoping that stupid Eric would see that I had done my homework and was in the loop more than he thought.

"We're us," Finn assured. "We'll be more careful. Besides, these aren't bombs, just small incendiary devices."

"What's the difference?" I asked.

"A few hundred pounds of dynamite," Vray said. "We're much lower tech. Water bottles full of gas with wicks."

"Yeah, but won't the cars explode after they catch fire?" I visualized the pop, pop, pop, bang followed by the wall of flames.

"Hopefully," Eric said. "And I'm not totally sold on the low-tech approach. I think we should look into timing devices. Plant 'em and run."

"I'll do another web search," Finn offered. "If we can put something together with untraceable parts from a dollar store or something, we could reconsider."

"Remember, only at the reference library on a drop-in computer," Vray said. "Never at home."

And so they went, on and on. Like they were doing a school project or planning a canoe trip or sharing cookie recipes. Except they were sharing a recipe for destruction. If O-Zone ever made a CD, that could be the title, a thought that almost made me laugh.

And that was about the only thing that kept me from crying.

• • •

"I always knew you'd do it," Vray said after the guys had left to do more planning. "That you'd do whatever it takes."

"How? I didn't even know."

"Because I know you better than you know yourself."

I probably should have been flattered. His remark was so intense and knowing, like some powerful declaration of love.

Instead it made me squirm.

"I've gotta go," I said, kissing him quickly as he saw me to the door.

"Remember, we only talk about this face to face. No phones, emails, nothing," he said, tugging on my braided pigtail.

"Cone of silence," I answered. "I get it."

"I know you do," he said softly. "That's what I love about you. You totally get it, me, the cause, all of it."

I nodded and walked toward the street to catch my bus home. And as I rewound the long, complicated memory spool of our relationship, I realized that in many ways I did get him but in so many others he was a complete stranger.

After all, he'd once been Matthew Rudolph, spoiled private school boy with clever but ridiculously busy intellectual parents. So what if he insisted he was also Vray Foret, high school guy, musician, eco-warrior? Just because he'd created this new, radical, green persona for himself didn't mean he actually inhabited it.

Maybe he snuck into Mickey Dees once in a while to cheat on his vegan diet. Or shopped for Made in China boxers and socks at Wal-Mart. Or left the tap running when he brushed his teeth.

I mean, I knew as well as anyone that full on green and clean living was difficult. And for all I knew, Vray's beat-up second-hand leather jacket was like that school blazer Ruby said he'd worn when he was younger. All about image instead of integrity.

When I really thought about it, it was pretty obvious that I didn't know Vray at all. I didn't really, truly know him. Not deep down. And it's not that I wasn't completely interested or absolutely in love with him or didn't try to find out every single solitary thing there was to know.

It's just, how can you begin to know someone else when you barely know yourself?

e a r t h g i r l
[Jan 28th | 06:14pm]
[mood | focused]
[music | mazzy star - fade into you]

earthgirl

THE MORE YOU KNOW THE LESS YOU NEED.
— Aboriginal saying, seen on a bumper sticker stuck to a bike fender.

It's soooo beautiful. Unfortunately, there will always be so much more that we don't know than we do know. So really, we will always NEED to know more.

I only hope that kind of NEED is okay.

link   read 3 | post
www.planetfriendly.net

"What happened to hip, hip, hoo-Vray?" Dad asked. "Your mom said he was coming for dinner."

"He's busy," I said, even though the truth was I hadn't invited him.

I just couldn't bear the thought of him making happy talk with the parents while silently plotting nefarious eco-attack-tics and groping me under the table. It was too deviant to make things seem huggy when they were FUBARed.

"Too bad. We haven't seen him for a while," Mom said, unpacking the bags of Thai take-out.

"I said he was busy, okay? He has a life, you know."

"You're a total hottie hog," Clare blurted. "Bet you didn't even give him the CD I burned for him."

She was right. There was way too much going on for some perky aside like, *"Hey babe, I know you've got arson on the brain and yes, I absolutely am seriously ready to go for it and oh yeah, Clare thought you might like this lame band!"* On top of that, I didn't want to encourage her annoying little crush on my boyfriend. Bad enough she always grabbed the phone when it rang and chatted him up before passing it to me.

With everything happening right now, the last thing I needed was her snooping into my business. Our business. So I ignored her and her stupidity as much as possible. The way I was ignoring and avoiding the units.

"Give this a zap, honey, will you?" Dad said, passing Clare a container of food. Clare scooted up from the table and plopped it into the microwave.

"Not in the Styrofoam," I huffed. "It's toxic."

"Toxic this," Clare answered, flipping me the bird.

"It's fine, Sabine," Dad said. "It just needs twenty seconds."

I let out a long dramatic sigh. Wouldn't these people ever learn?

"Mr. Butler called," Mom said casually. Too casually. "And I felt a bit stupid not knowing about the D on your math test."

"No big deal," I said. "It was one little test."

"But you've been doing so well lately," Mom said. "Your A plus then suddenly this? It's a bit schizo, honey."

"We can get you a tutor," Dad said with his mouth full.

"I had period cramps and I choked. That's all. I'm not flunking, promise."

"Okay, if you say so. But remember, D is for the doghouse and we don't want you there," Dad said.

"Yeah, I get it," I said, digging in the bag for chopsticks even though the meal wasn't veggie, or organic, or even in recyclable containers. I was famished. And not in the mood to talk.

"Speaking of choking, carnage on the court today. Stan Stewart played like he was drunk, which he might actually have been," Dad gloated. "So you lucky ladies are dining with a semifinalist."

"Way to go, Dad," Clare cheered.

"Yeah, congrats," I chimed in, like there was nothing more exciting in the universe than my dad advancing in a rinky-dink squash tournament.

His face lit up like fireworks he was so thrilled. And suddenly the slipping grades and pending delinquency of their eldest daughter were forgotten as we all celebrated his small victory and mawed down like we'd never seen food before.

Faking out my parents was getting way too easy. I wondered if maybe it was a sign or cosmic wink or something. A sign that with careful consideration and the right preparation, maybe anything, however outrageous and radical and extreme it may seem on the surface, was actually possible.

And meant to be.

e a r t h g i r l
[Feb. 2nd | 11:38pm]
[mood | numb]
[music | this mess we're in – PJ Harvey with Thom Yorke]

How sad is it that eco-activists and earthkeepers have to

hide and cover their faces when they head out in public to defend the mother earth. As if they should be ashamed of knowing and doing what's right. And in need of protecting.

Shouldn't the greedy C-E-Os who put profit ahead of the planet be the ones hiding? Instead they're practically celebrities. The world has seriously gone crazy.

link   read 4 | post

lacklusterlulu 02-02 22:42
I'm not crazy. And neither are you. So let's save the world sis-tah!
www.wwf.ca

Vague-a-bond 02-03 01:01
I'll help in anyway I can and promise do my very best (and least) every single day.

I was in charge of getting gloves, balaclavas and nonde-script packs. Vray had given me a hundred bucks (in small bills he'd had broken at a corner store, "just in case") to get everything on the memorized list. They wanted everything on hand if we moved up the plan. So the next day after school, I took the subway and streetcar to Kensington Market.

Amidst the food stalls and second-hand boutiques were a bunch of rag-tag shops that sold reflective construction-worker vests, knitted dockworker toques, woolie socks and other sensible low-tech stuff. Basically everything necessary to disguise us so we could wreak havoc and make our grand environmental statement.

Instead I found myself wandering into one of those old-style taverns and ordering a beer. I didn't even think I liked beer, but it felt like the thing to do at that particular moment. The moment when I felt more like an actor in a movie than a sixteen-year-old wannabe activist trainwreck. So really, I wasn't surprised when the grizzled guy behind the bar deposited a bottle in front of me without blinking. Maybe he knew I was underage and didn't care. At this point it was the least of my law-breaking activities.

I moved to a seat by the window to watch the world go by. The students with their loaded book bags, the spiky tattooed punkers with their snarling doggies, the old shuffling Asian ladies towing bundle buggies, the hardworking storekeepers. All those strangers going about their lives, totally clueless about the person right beside them. Or watching them. Or maybe even their wife, or kids, or brother, or neighbor, or dad.

I mean, if we could put on a quasi-costume and fool ourselves into behaving like other people, how hard could it be to fool everyone else?

I took a sip of the beer. It tasted cold and sour in my mouth.

twenty_

"What's all this?" Vray asked as I dumped a few cans of spraypaint from my pack onto his bed.

"Our supplies," I announced.

"We're not tagging anything. We're in and we're out," he explained. "If we want cred, we'll post a manifesto on the E-L-F site after." He poked around in my pack and pulled out the two balaclavas I'd also bought. "Where's the rest of the stuff? There are four of us."

"No, there are two," I answered. "Me and you. I'll make a bunch of U-SUX posters. I've got gloves, glue and spraypaint but that's as far as it goes."

"You're kidding, right?" he said. "This is just nerves, right, babe? Trust me, they'll pass. They always do."

"No. This is the plan. My plan. The only plan."

"Or what? You'll call it off?" he laughed. He went to his desk, grabbed a stack of photos of the dealership and handed them to me. "We've spent a ton of time planning this, scouting, taking pictures, playing out scenarios, looking at every angle the way we do every time."

"What other times?" I asked calmly, both curious and terrified.

"You in or out?"

"I'm calling it off," I said flatly, suddenly realizing the whole adventure had taken on a life of its own and was raging out of control. And I needed to take that control back. No matter what it took.

"You can't," he said. "It's not up to you."

"Yes I can and I am."

"You do and we're done," he answered quietly.

"Go through with it and we're done," I snapped back, feeling suddenly strong and absolutely, totally right.

"You don't mean that," he said suddenly, defensive.

"Stop telling me what I mean and what I want and who I am. Just stop it already!"

"I'm not, I just…" He stared at me, and for the first time since I'd known him I saw confusion in his eyes.

"Look, I don't know what kind of whacked superhero shit you did before we met, or what else you have cooking and I can't do anything about that," I said, letting out a long, slow breath. "But this was my idea, my idea you twisted into something ugly and wrong and I'm taking it back."

"Okay, fine, we'll just do spraypaint. This time. Get you ready and practice for the real deal."

"No, I changed my mind. We won't do any of it. No paint, no anything. Were you even listening?"

"I've been listening for a long time. Long enough to know there's a war going on out there and we're all part of it," he replied, like what he was saying made complete sense instead of being total bullshit. "And now's the time to step up or shut up."

"I'm not fighting the same fight as you."

"Yes, you are. You just won't admit it," he snapped.

"This is done, Vray. We're finished."

It took saying it out loud like that for me to realize it was true. And strangely enough, instead of feeling freaked or upset, I felt relieved.

I went over to his bed, shoveled the spraycans into my pack and hooked it over my arm.

I looked at him one last time. I wanted to memorize all the great things about him. I wanted to remember that even if right now he was a bit confused and cocky, deep down he was also sweet, caring, intelligent and fun. That his intentions were probably good even if his expressions weren't.

"We were really good there, for a while," I said as I closed the door behind me.

e a r t h g i r l
[Feb. 06th | 12:53pm]
[mood | You name it, I'm feeling it!]
[music | – ?! at a time like this?!]

Mahatma Gandhi, the great teacher and man of peace and justice once said:

"You must be the change you wish to see in the world."

And since I have a ton of ideas and innovations, but no motto per se, I've decided that's going to be mine. My womanifesto. My eco-ethos. To lead by example and help the world be a nicer, kinder, gentler, cleaner, calmer, better and happier place.

I WILL BE THE CHANGE I WISH TO SEE IN THE WORLD.

I don't know if I can change much. But I can change myself.

link   post comment
www.epec.org

After retreating to bed and spending two bleary and teary-eyed days under my duvet, I figured I had to get back into the world. Plus another day in the fog of my mind and fug of my room and my mom would drag me to the doctor, which given the way pills were handed out like candy might lead to medicated mediation.

And now, more than ever, I needed to stay clear.

It wasn't easy. I felt pukey and restless and completely on edge. As if the incredibly debilitating sadness and exhaustion weren't enough, I was paranoid I might bump into Vray at the co-op. Or worse, his pack might try to infiltrate my school to intercept and hound or harass or berate me. I knew it wasn't likely. Then again, I also thought I knew a lot more than I apparently did.

I didn't dare call the car dealership back after my initial pay-phone-dialed warning (it was tough enough finding a public phone). And sneaking past to see if they'd reconfigured their cameras or hired extra security was out of the question. So if something had happened, I hadn't heard about it on the radio or seen it online. Which in an odd way I had mixed feelings about.

Then again, at this particular moment, all of my feelings were decidedly mixed and mixed up.

"Ah-ha, you're here," Shane nodded as I walked past his sentry post by the stoner tree.

"What's that supposed to mean?"

"That you're here," he shrugged. "And didn't run off with the E-L-F or relocate to a tree."

I didn't know whether to be impressed or horrified.

"Should I know you by any other name?" I asked, wondering if Shane could be altalake, lorax, earthbound01 or even possibly onederful.

"I'm more an observer, not much for the blah-blah," he said, shaking his head. "Unlike most of the goofs around here, I don't need to express an opinion about everything. I've got nothing to prove." And with a bow of his beautiful dreaded-head, he turned and walked toward the school doors.

"Am I imagining it or are you and Shane McCardle getting tight?" Ella squealed as she snuck up behind me. As if there had never been a blip in our friendship. "Watch yourself, girlie. Va-va-va-Vray's gonna be seriously jealous."

"Doubtful," I answered softly. Then after a moment I added, "We're not together anymore."

"Shut up!" she shrieked. "Did he dump you?"

"No," I sighed, suddenly exhausted. "Another time, okay? It's complicated."

231   **earthgirl**

"Well, he's a total idiot cause you're completely awesome, Bean," she said. It was actually quite sweet. "Though he's definitely a supreme hottie."

Incendiary even. Something I instantly extinguished by standing up for myself when things got too heated.

But if I just dove into the cosmic jet stream of life instead of deciding things myself, where would that take me? If I didn't think or care about the consequences of my actions, I could end up anywhere. Kicked out of school, in juvie or even dead. And really, how useful was I going to be in any of those places?

"You okay, Bean?" Ella asked as she touched my arm. "I didn't upset you about him, did I?"

"No, I'm fine," I said as I headed toward the school. "I'm good."

And as the words came out of my mouth tangled with puffs of condensation in the cold, clear morning, I knew it was true.